DEVON LIBRARIES

Please return/renew this item by the due date.
Renew on tel. 0845 155 1001 or at
www.devonlibraries

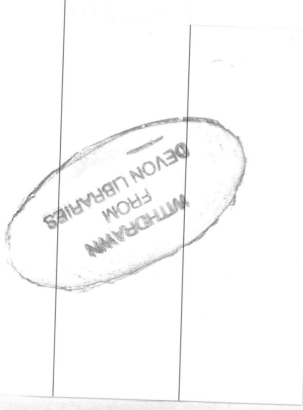

A PERFECT ENDING

AND OTHER STORIES

Vivien Varga

Matador
Unit E2 Airfield Business Park,
Harrison Road, Market Harborough,
Leicestershire. LE16 7UL
Tel: 0116 2792299
Email: books@troubador.co.uk
Web: www.troubador.co.uk/matador
Twitter: @matadorbooks

ISBN 978 1803135 489

British Library Cataloguing in Publication Data.
A catalogue record for this book is available from the British Library.

Printed and bound in Great Britain by 4edge Limited
Typeset in 12pt Minion Pro by Troubador Publishing Ltd, Leicester, UK

Matador is an imprint of Troubador Publishing Ltd

For my darling boys. x

CONTENTS

A PERFECT ENDING

ONE

Wisdom of mountains. Trees trickle down their sides thickly, like a verdant, velvet robe. A comfortingly warm fluidity. The mountains protect, calmly leaning over named boxes of tourist accommodation – Vista Mar, Neptune Apartamentos – which in their own way form a notable part of this panorama, this unity. The bare beaches first come alive in spring when tourists are sewn into the sand with fluorescent parasols, like mushrooms, shining forth luminescence... magic.

Problems which have gnawed relentlessly for weeks, months, years, decades, melt away here. 'No problem! No problem!' Great mantra!

The salt-seasoned sea receives its abundant rush of yellow liquid accompanied by guilty looks: *we know you did it*, say the little bubbles gathering around the offending citizen for all to see.

People, canoes, slide boats, motorboats all form a pattern which, if joined together like a dot-to-dot puzzle, could well resemble an octopus, dolphin – shark! Be careful, it's divine retribution for peeing in the ocean! And take note, when swimming be sure there's an oblivious human further out to sea than you, for fear keen white fangs lurk in the distance, under the surface, ready to strike.

Fish nibble at the shiny silver nail varnish of an unsuspecting woman who screams unnecessarily into the air, scaring other bathers. And out of the blue, a piercingly painful prick punctures someone's foot, causing a swelling almost as big as a balloon, given the fuss! The mountains sigh and the wise woman from the village becomes their mouthpiece. Don't make a mountain out of a molehill. "Pee on it," she says. The man does and it works! More magic! This really is the place of dreams.

Buildings like distressed Lego line the promenade, punctuated by bars, restaurants, ice-cream parlours. And freshly showered, perfumed groups in newly purchased gaudy attire stroll to souvenir shops and buy brash vases, which are frowned on once home, and local honey which leaks in the overloaded case.

Brand-new couples, keen to impress, hold hands and drift into brightly lit bars where they eagerly sip sophisticated emerald-gold cocktails at exaggerated prices. Vintage ladies with minute candyfloss dogs in pink bows slowly mix and merge into the noisy crowd. Solo individuals soak up the scenery before choosing a local bar or coffee shop to read a well-thumbed book from a charity store. And there she is. The girl in a tie-dyed T-shirt, denim shorts, bumbag, and novel held closely by her side. Lisa, that's her name, or it should be because she looks like a Lisa, with cropped brown hair, grey-blue eyes and, so far, pale skin. She must have just arrived.

"Excuse me," she asks. "Could you tell me where the plaza is? I heard they were selling local street food."

"Sure, follow me," replies the man. Funny that. The town is crowded. Yet she chooses him. She likes his dark, tousled hair… and soft voice. And she wants to be with him. Just for the afternoon. Maybe more. So, they buy bocadillos and he leads her through ancient, paint-peeled, once-grand gates and up creaking wooden stairs with too much give, to his cosy little room on the top floor.

"*Hola*, Señora Alegría!"[1] he calls suddenly into mid-air. And Lisa giggles.

"*Puta*,"[2] spits a gruff old lady from across the hall as she presses her eye to the tiny, all-observing peephole carved into a tired, flimsy door which is no stranger to slamming.

Lisa is an art student. Do all art students wear plimsolls? Lisa does anyway. She has some pictures to sell. Of orange sunsets and bright-blue seas. People buy these and display them on off-white walls in cold countries.

"Pablo!" shouts an agitated woman hanging, like sun-flushed honeysuckle, from a doorway. "Get in now!" She projects well due to much practice. "Dinner is cold!" But he's busy, proud to be seen with older boys who have a skateboard with skulls. He is embarrassed when she calls him and pretends she isn't there. The woman *will* be heard and rushes out, tugging his ear, pinching his cheek, turning his olive skin red.

---

1   Alegría – happiness.
2   Puta (derogatory) – street girl, prostitute.

A lazy cat sprawls out on the warm, golden sand like an unrolled rug. Its eyes are slits, and it purrs contentment. A happy life. Lots of sun. Lots of fish. It's glad to live here. Who wouldn't be?

Lisa's happy too. The man has dimples when he smiles, and she doesn't feel alone. Her step is light. She eats tacos from a van and watches children on scooters and ladies chatting with their mouths and arms and hands. And vendors in their stalls tidy the pile of jumpers disturbed by tourists who touch but don't buy. This is not allowed on the fruit stall, where an all-seeing, aproned woman, hands on hips, stands guard. *Don't you dare*, she says with her eyes. Terrified tourists won't have fruit with their picnic today. But the locals buy. They know her bark is worse than her bite. "*Hola*, Margarita!" and she melts into a smile, ruining her ferociousness.

Lisa shares her food with a stray dog. And places her paintings on the pavement.

"Oh, how lovely. That would brighten up the lounge," says rosy-cheeked Elsa from Sweden.

Lisa is delighted. She has sold two paintings today to enthusiastic people who will love them. Like she will love this dog. Artists like dogs. Well, Lisa does anyway. It is bedraggled and flea-bitten but now its troubles seem over. The landlady won't have dogs, so Lisa leaves and sleeps on the beach. And in the morning, there he is. The man. With two coffees and jam bollos.

"I saw you from the promenade," he says simply.

"Thanks for the breakfast. The landlady won't have dogs," comes her matter-of-fact response.

"You can stay with me." And he means it. He likes Lisa. And dogs.

"We can give this one a bath and buy some flea-killer."

And later, man and dog pose for a picture. And she draws his dimples (the man's) and green eyes and lives for the now.

Pablo is in trouble again. He has fallen off the big boys' skateboard and gashed his leg and ripped his trousers. His mother does not have money for more. She tenderly bathes his wound while causing his ear to vibrate with her scolding. And he wants a skateboard for Christmas. Or some earplugs!

A sweet old lady buys Lisa's painting of man and dog. Everyone strokes the dog who now holds his head high in the plaza.

And when, two weeks later, Lisa boards the plane, the wise mountains smile. The dog has a home and the man a new purpose. And, maybe, Lisa will return one day.

TWO

'Looking out of the window in a dark, empty room. Create a state of solitude and gloom, contrasted with light and hope.'

And, for this assignment, Lisa had depicted the musty, mustard walls of her flat with its dim, dark-grey lamps and, out of the window, a bright-orange light lounging on a blue horizon.

And two years on, she had returned to Spain. The ever-patient mountains saw the girl and wondered... would she shy away – or stay for a perfect ending?

Perched on a wall by the tourist-coated beach, she fixes her gaze on a tiny lizard, who stands stone-still for a second before shooting like a flash into an accommodating hole in a small rock nearby. And Lisa hadn't noticed the cat who now paws frustratedly at the minute gap in the hard surface and sits... watching, waiting... for the creature to re-emerge to meet its untimely fate.

Mice are far easier prey, laments the feline inwardly. And it falls asleep, oblivious of the canny reptile stealing soundlessly past its twitching nose.

On the ocean's surface, pulsing golden flecks dance in the sunlight forming an ever-widening passage to the sandy, shell-strewn shore. And she is glad to be here. Glad to be back. Glad to feel free again.

"*Agua, agua, agua!*" shouts the vendor like a demented duck, as he plods with difficulty, feet sinking ever deeper into the soft, hot sand. "*Agua, agua, agua!*" as he grips the heavy basket supporting his watery load. Can you believe it? There are still some who recklessly discard the plastic bottle after their thirst is quenched. And the bin is just metres away! Do humans ever learn?!

And, coming into view, led by the excitable dog along the pink-paved promenade, is the man, who, ready to rest his tired legs, soon slumps down on a sun-baked wall, next to a small, sugar-coated child cheerfully chewing his last scrap of churro. And the dog knows that this is pretty much it for the day. So, lazily, he stretches out on the hot ground, ogling the ice cream being tantalisingly slurped by greedy gobblers, who lick the melting stream running in irregular lines down the cone like lava from a volcano.

"Where does your abundant energy hail from, Pepe?" says his doting master. "We've been racing around all day; even the ball's exhausted. I'm ready for a siesta." And after this well-deserved pause, the duo melt into the crowd and drift home.

"Pablo, come here! Dinner is ready! I won't tell you again! All you do is play, play, play – on that wood on wheels! When you gonna do homework? When, huh, when?" shouts his exhausted mother who simply cannot talk quietly for love nor money.

And the boy, several centimetres taller now, hurriedly picks up his skateboard, dotingly tucking it under his arm.

"Coming, Mama!" No ear-pulling needed today.

School is not for Pablo, but he has a passion for art, and his teacher, Señor Rodríguez... Pedro... the man, is his favourite by far. He motivates Pablo. Inspires him. And Pablo wishes to become an artist. His mother wants him to work in the local bank as it is a job with a pension. And just down the road.

Funny that Lisa picked this man. Pedro. An artist like her. Funny. Fate maybe.

She sees him the next day, paddling in the sea, and calls his name. His face lights up. The dog bounds over and licks Lisa's cheek. He remembers her kindness – of course he does. And her body radiates warmth as she watches Pedro approach. His smile welcomes her. Those beautiful dimples. And she is home. Home.

The omnipresent mountains breathe constancy, calm. Pedro and Lisa... somehow a match made in heaven. With adoring dog in tow. Pepe.

And Pablo paints his mother. She feels special posing on a wicker chair, a light shawl draped over her shoulders. He conveys her assertiveness. He makes her skin soft with his watercolours. She is pleased. And kisses him.

And the cat basks in the sun. Mice have more meat on them than lizards anyway.

And Lisa stays. Of course she does. And the sun hugs the mountains, and the gentle waves kiss the shore.

LIFE ON THE EDGE

S he sat stock-still in the boardroom, pinned to a chair, heart beating frantically against her ribcage like an incarcerated inmate desperate for reprieve.

Her spirit was crushed. The endless, murky bog she constantly tried to negotiate, dragged her down. Now, submerged in muddy waters, she only occasionally managed to reach the surface but was forever swimming against the tide.

Cold, marble faces, solid – carved like an icy mountain range – threatened from the opposite side of the table. Motionless. Inaccessible. Sterile. And she was a landslide, a victim ready for the chop. Then it came. The dreaded question.

"What is your opinion on the matter, Elsa?"

How could she possibly know? She hadn't been in the room. Well physically, yes, but mentally she had been sucked into a dank quagmire, drowning, suffocating at the bottom of a dark ditch in a world which defied all logic. The talk of the last hour might as well have been voiced in an alien tongue. All that had registered was a mumbling discordant chorus of nothingness.

"Uh… um…" came the broken utterance, as her cheeks flamed scarlet. Pathetic. Her palms were moist, her head ringing like a shrill alarm. The humiliation was excruciating.

Her boss, inexpertly masking acute irritation, said: "OK. Let's move on. We'll come back to you later. Maybe you should take some fresh air."

They simply had not the slightest idea about her life.

That morning, the best part of an hour had been required for her to descend the twenty-five stairs in her house before reaching the bottom. Distressing imaginings had invaded her mind and their cruel, brutal advance was relentless. This destructive onslaught had to be neutralised by positive mantra in order for her to move on; but to win the battle was not so easy, as negative thoughts flooded through, like a dam bursting its banks, and to concentrate on positive affirmations, thus keeping the dam intact, was all-consuming. So, when she finally arrived in utter exhaustion at the foot of the stairs, she was late for work and ready to cry. And it was only 9am. There would be nigh on a thousand intrusions throughout the course of the week. So, when her colleagues bade her good morning, they really had no idea, that actually it hadn't been thus far. And might not be for the rest of the day. Or the next day. Or the next. For this *dis-ease* was unyielding and had been for years. A hostile adversary residing deep inside of her – a parasite.

And the mask she used to hide behind was fast becoming threadbare.

"There's a party tomorrow. Do you want to come, Elsa? All the office are going."

No! came the inner scream. "Yes, thank you. That

sounds fun," she said. How could she get out of it? She really must avoid this looming ordeal.

"Great. See you there." Carol was pleasant if a tad irksome. She rounded up the strays in an effort to include everyone, without considering that not everyone wanted to be included.

Switch the lights on off, on off, on off, on off. Shut, open, shut, open, shut the door. Think nice thoughts. I will die if I touch the doorknob again. Die. So, I must not. Until tomorrow at 8.30am, but not a minute before. This is not real. Not real. Not real. Wash my hands once more.

Elsa's hands were rough like sandpaper. Her sparkly party dress was far, far too hopeful. The taxi came. She had to find a way of saying 'hello' three times for luck or her cat would disappear forever under the wheels of a car. How could she do this without sounding weird? But she was weird. No doubt about it.

"Hello," she said, awkwardly climbing onto the back seat. And five minutes later: "Hello, what's that?"

"What?" replied the cabbie.

"Oh, a massive dog the size of a horse," she lied. "It's gone now."

"Here we are," he said.

"Hello... I mean goodbye."

He gave her a strange look. Unsurprisingly, she often received quizzical glances.

Sometimes, in the street, she would freeze as negatives had to be replaced by positives before she could continue. *Stop, die... go, live... stop, stop, stop... no! Go... stop. Go!*

What was wrong with her? She was an intelligent woman. Why couldn't she find a way to free her mind, unchain her brain?

After greeting her colleagues, Elsa hurriedly made for a table in a shady corner of the venue in the hope she would be less conspicuous. Sadly, this worked for a mere moment until *too-keen-by-far* Adrian found her.

"Hi Elsa, so great you're here. I love your dress. May I join you? Let me buy you a drink. What's your tipple?"

"Oh, no need. Thanks anyway." And her safe place, like a stamped-on sandcastle, crumbled. *Go away Adrian – go away. For pity's sake!* But the man, steadfast, was not intending to budge any time soon.

"I'll get you a surprise cocktail. Leave it to me. Won't be long. You'll love it, I promise." And, undeterred and overeager, he made for the bar.

The girl froze. *I can't do this. I can't do this.*

The tacky, gaudy coloured drink in a thick-stemmed glass, with plastic seahorse basking under a pink-tinsel parasol, soon found its way to the waiting table. Proudly, he placed it in front of her and the offering, like a peacock's feathers, conveyed sexual interest.

"Now try this. It's a blend of orange liqueur and…"

It's poison. Poison. Poison. He wants to kill me. I'm dead unless… tap the table ten times and say 'thank you' five. Tap the table.

"Thank you, thank you." Tap, tap, tap.

"My pleasure."

"Thank you. Thank you."

"You've already thanked me."

"Thank you."

Here it was. The familiar bemused look. Questioning. Tap, tap, tap. Tap, tap, tap.

"Are you OK, Elsa? Why are you tapping the table?"

"Oh, this?" Tap. *Done! Now spill the drink. He's trying to kill you.*

"Oh no. I'm so sorry! Forgive me."

"I'll fetch a cloth." And off he went, limply, only a fraction put out.

This was her chance. Grabbing her handbag, she dashed desperately out of the venue and into the dark street, where a taxi was hailed; and her pounding heart beat evermore rapidly in her chest, like a fox fleeing hounds.

Once home, the girl unlocked the door with trembling hands and threw herself onto the sofa where she stayed until sleep, like morphine, calmed her, briefly setting her free.

And come morning, before the drowsiness waned, Elsa bathed in heavenly calm – a luxury beyond all compare. That is, until she recalled there would be a visit from her friend, with a tiny, yet deadly, child in tow. Germs. Germs on his small, dirty hands; liquorice breath, black-stained lips and filthy shoes. Maybe he had stepped in dogs' mess? Her carpets would be soiled, contaminated, stinking! Mucky, sticky little paws with infinite impurities would touch all her surfaces, invade all her cupboards, smother her clean sanctuary in invisible grime. *Oh no!* In her mind, she could not see the child, just the hazard and nothing more. Nothing.

"Shall I help you take off your shoes, Max?"

"Don't want to."

"Well, it might be a good idea," she persisted.

"Don't want to."

"Leave him, Elsa. He's fine. They're clean."

No! No, they are most certainly not! "OK, as you wish."

And he didn't want to wash his hands either. This was exposure in the extreme. Life was exposure. She was helpless... again. Afraid. Out of her comfort zone. Out of control.

The afternoon trudged on and on, and she observed from the outside all the terrifying events which unfolded in front of her eyes during the three horrendous hours she had been forced to endure, until eventually, the two left. *Thank God!* They had no idea what they had done. *None!*

The following *ten* hours, no less, saw her scrubbing, washing, disinfecting and sobbing, sobbing her heart out. This was just another all-too-familiar day.

And why, on God's earth, was she afraid of hair? Not her own but unidentified individual strands. She had taken a coat to be dry-cleaned and, on receiving the supposedly pristine garment, had spotted a hair, a stranger's hair. When this problem – and it was a *huge* problem – had been broached, the man laughed off her complaint with the words: "It's probably mine, love! Happens all the time. Must be getting old." And, as he nonchalantly brushed away the offending strand, his smile revealed stained, yellowing teeth, which further aggravated her terror, thus inducing, in her mind's eye, myriads of hairs to latch with leech-like resolve onto the now contaminated material.

After hurriedly depositing the coat in the boot of her car, Elsa had squirted her hands with antiviral gel over twenty times – 'will these hands ne'er be clean?', and we all know the answer to that one! The coat had remained in the vehicle for six whole weeks before, with thick rubber gloves clinging to her shaking hands, she had plucked up the courage to remove it and throw it in the bin.

"You're bonkers!" said her friend Amy, the honest one. "That was a dope coat – boucle's all the rage now!"

Other reactions when she mentioned certain of her behavioural traits were as follows: 'All will be fine. Just think of the people less fortunate than you', which, translated, means: *For God's sake, pull yourself together!* Then, just as awful, those who offered pity: 'Oh you *poor, poor* thing!' And she most certainly did not want pity. Why would she want that? A cure, remedy, solution maybe, just not this sprinkling of trite, two a penny platitudes. But folk looked at her differently. All the time. Differently. And once, she had delivered a well-received speech at the office, which had prompted the comment (spoken with a sugary lilt): 'Now aren't you a little star, Elsa!', patronising even to a child. She had wanted to respond with an appropriate rebuff but instead smiled and sat quietly seething and, at the same time, sad.

Always lurking, lurking in the shadows, the dark recesses of her mind, were thoughts which lingered, ready to lunge and attach with claw-clinging certainty to her defenceless being and chew away at her sanity.

Anything could trigger a panic attack – maybe stress, maybe something out of the blue which, for no known reason, would emerge to torment her. Whatever the case, she would freeze, and destructive thoughts would fly into her head and crawl through her brain, like invading ants. Fear would cause her chest to pound and heave, rendering breathing laboured and her body tight. It was always imperative to place good over bad. Good over bad. *I will live and be healthy. No, I will die! No, no. Live. Die. Live. Die. Live, live, live!*

"Are you alright dear?"

No!

"Um, yes. Fine thanks." *Die. Live, live, live!*

"Are you sure? I could fetch some water. You look so pale."

"Really, I'm fine." *Go away, please go!* Just another day.

Numbers too were a problem; they had to be even, because this ensured safety from hideous death. Odd numbers were forbidden. Purchases in the supermarket were added carefully to ensure an even total and she would panic dreadfully if there were an offer which changed the final amount. In the event of this happening, she would buy something else to create an over-all even number. These rituals had to be completed otherwise there would be an acute thumping of the chest and racing heartbeat, but they were becoming ever more time-consuming, ever harder.

A visit to the doctor had her return home with several elastic bands round her wrist.

"Whenever you have unpleasant thoughts, just twang the bands hard and say: 'Stop!'," he had concluded. Such wisdom!

A few weeks later, she had been forced to return to the surgery as her wrists were infected. Strong antidepressants had then been prescribed, which had numbed her completely, transforming her into a lobotomised zombie. And, unsurprisingly, after a lengthy sick leave, she had been sacked.

Every day she suffered. Her *dis-ease* was misunderstood by all, with the best will in the world, misunderstood. So, she internalised her strife. Her private hell. Silently. Further and further away she drifted… each day further, until she was the only person on her planet.

And one sunny afternoon, she found herself driving to Cornwall. A comfortable guesthouse near the coast had been chosen with apt decorations: anchors, porcelain seagulls, rope fishing nets and ornate shells. A bottle of white wine had been consumed, at a little wooden table, accompanied by a portion of fish and chips. And afterwards she had retired to her room and slept soundly until daylight.

That morning she ventured to the seafront, where happy tourists tumbled out of brightly painted beach huts, gladly spilling like extra ingredients onto the finely sifted, silk sands. And she sat watching them… couples, families, children… observing their laughter, games, connection. And when, at the end of the day, all had left and she was completely alone, she walked calmly towards the beckoning sea. And waded, waded into the welcoming waves.

Elsa wasn't afraid of water.

THE CHAIR

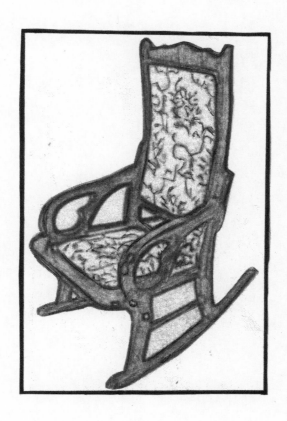

S ilently enduring. Permanent. The chair had witnessed and absorbed the joy, sorrow, fear of numerous generations: grandmothers, grandfathers, mothers, fathers, daughters, sons. It was an all-present icon. Ubiquitous. Eternal.

One (1914)

"Why must my son go to war? The only son I have. Sending him to the trenches, to a certain death, is a heinous crime."

"Darling, we have no choice, and you know that. No choice at all. He wants to fight for his country. So that we'll all be free. He will go without our permission."

"Oh God. I fear for his life. You hear such dreadful stories. I feel so helpless. I see him as a young child at the beach, searching for crabs in the rock pools, his fishing net full of shells, and paddling in the ripples with his little toes splashing. That tiny freckle on his left cheek… so beautiful. And that innocent smile. I see his fine, golden hair ruffled by the breeze. And his silky, smooth

face on the flannelette pillow with soft eyes closed…
dreaming, drifting, to another place. I love him with
all my heart. How can I send him to a godforsaken
wilderness? How can I?"

"Darling, he's a man. Not a boy any longer. Many
men go to war to defend their country. Many men suffer
the trenches. Many men. He wants to go – to fight, for
all our sakes. To fight for our freedom."

"But why my child? My only son. My flesh."

"It's hard, but we are powerless to change the course
of events. You know that. Don't cry, dry your tears."

"I thank God our daughter will be spared. But I feel
faint, let me sit… the chair is so comforting and warm,
like an embrace."

**

"Do you remember the last time we visited Auntie?
All those years ago, a few months before she died. We
sat drinking tea and eating Eccles cakes."

"Yes, I remember. And we talked about Uncle
Charlie's copper kettle – the only thing he ever made;
how proud he was – and their runner beans and
raspberries and lavender bushes awash with cabbage
whites and red admirals."

"And bumble bees. Yes, and Danny wanted lavender,
to invite butterflies and bees to our garden. The bushes
are still there, not so many butterflies now though…
now he's gone. Remember his bear, Archibald – Archi?
It's on the windowsill in his room. Oh, I cannot stand
this emptiness, this void."

"I know, darling. But what happened belongs to the past now. And for our own sanity we must leave it there. We cannot change a thing. What's done is done. Then was not a time to be sentimental. His country needed him."

"Yes, so said all the billboards: 'Your country needs you!' It makes me shudder thinking about it. Do you remember when he was bullied by those boys at school, and it took him a whole month to tell us? He came home with black eyes, bloody nose and was too terrified to say who had inflicted his wounds for fear his daily torment would escalate. I want to bathe those wounds now... all of them."

"He was such a sensitive soul. So delicate."

"Yes. He should have been an artist. A painter. Not a soldier. Oh, why did I let him sign up?"

"There's no point berating yourself. No point. You couldn't have stopped him. He joined up, he fought for king and country. And, sadly, like many others, he perished."

"Reading that telegram was agony. A part of me died too, that day."

"Yes. I know. But please don't torture yourself. Sit down, dear. Here's an extra cushion for the chair. I'll bring you some tea."

I absorb their daily grief as they stare with watery eyes at Danny's sepia photo on the shelf, its haunting presence like an open grave. They are unable to digest the reality of his death. Father constantly reassures in an overly calm voice, lacking any real conviction. Mother's aching heart will never mend, but she will adjust; she will have to. When she sits down, I want to offer words of comfort, a soothing poem perhaps, but my thoughts are silent, so I rock her in my arms to gently cushion her sorrow.

Two (1945)

"Get off me! You're hurting! I'll tell Mum! Ow!"

"You always tell Mum. Don't be such a baby."

"Stupid boy! You think you're so great, don't you! Untie me right now. You baboon!"

"Ooo, baboon! Strong words. You were the one who wanted to play 'Cops and Robbers', not me!"

"Yes, but the cops are supposed to tie up the robbers, not the other way round!"

"Things aren't always fair, Sis. Don't take it to heart. I won!"

"Well, I'm going to free myself. You just watch me!"

"Stop rocking, Sis, the chair will tilt. Stop it! Mary! – Mum! Mum! Mary's fallen, and she's banged her head on the table!"

"Mary! Darling! We need to call the doctor right away – she's unconscious. Quick! There are some coins on the table, James. Run to the telephone kiosk, as fast as you can! Hurry!"

***

"She has a twisted ankle and a large bump on her forehead, and her back is badly grazed, but nothing that a couple of weeks' rest won't mend. You need to play carefully, James. You are lucky she missed that stone hearth. You could have lost her. It's not a good idea tying people to chairs. When she fell, she couldn't put her hands out to break the fall."

"Don't worry, Doctor. It won't happen again. A lesson has been learnt, hasn't it, James?"

"Yes, Mum. Sorry."

"Alright, we'll say no more about it. Now go to your room. Let Mary sleep."

"And how is your husband, Mrs Gilbert?"

"He's so very depressed, Doctor. He sits all day in the chair looking out of the window, and cries. It's as if he feels guilty for surviving the war when so many of his comrades died."

"Yes, that's a common sentiment within the armed forces. His recovery will doubtless take time. One can only be patient and not expect too much."

"Certainly, and I try my best to be supportive where I can. I just thank God the war is finally over."

"I couldn't agree more. Take care of yourself."

"Thank you, I shall. Goodbye Doctor."

"Goodbye."

***

"Mary, may I come in? Do you feel better today?"

"Yes, a bit. Sit on the bed. Listen, I know this could

29

well seem silly, but I think the chair saved me; it spun round and changed direction, so my fall was broken."

"Haha, that's funny – and impossible, Sis. You're bored so your imagination's running wild. You're not thinking straight."

"I suppose you're right; it just seemed so very real. Will you read to me? *Little Women*, I am halfway through. There's a bookmark."

"*Little Women*? That's a girls' book! Do I have to?"

"Yes. I need to rest my head. It's a wonderful book. I love it. But pour me some water first."

"OK. Look, Sis. I'm sorry for what happened, believe me. I feel really guilty."

"So you should. But I forgive you. As long as you fetch, carry, read to me, brush my hair —"

"Brush your hair! Worse than prison! But I'll do it. OK, *Little Women* as requested. Ready?"

"Yes. Ready."

"But please don't tell my friends that I read to you – or that I brushed your hair."

"I'll think about it."

Kids will be kids! Running around like frolicking colts, they believe they are invincible, unbreakable, and their eyes sparkle with curiosity – so full of life, of hope. Just in time, I swivelled round so Mary's dear head would avoid hitting the marble hearth, and in so doing, a far, far graver injury was averted. Thankfully, her wounds healed quickly. James read the rest of Little Women *to his sister and secretly loved it! And Father rocked in*

my arms for two long years before he could release
all guilt and allow his tears to dry.

Three (2015)

"Shoo, Maxi, you great brute. I know you love this chair, but you're not allowed on it. Your fur will be all over the cushion. And stop looking at me with those sad eyes, which always melt my heart. Clever, that's what you are.

"And, Joe, get off that PlayStation! You've been on it all morning! We used to play Jacks or Rummy when I was your age, or Monopoly. But now, it's screen, screen, screen, all the time."

"Give me a break, Mum. I'm playing with Robby, and he's killed me twice so far. I need to fight back so I can earn enough points for a samurai sword! Then I'll win the war, and he'll be toast! Just a few more minutes – *please*, Mum. I love you!"

"Ha! Clever child too! But that game doesn't seem very friendly."

"Don't worry, Mum, it's not real."

"Mmm. Where's your father?"

"Gone to buy pizza for lunch."

"Very nutritious! I don't suppose it's a vegetarian option; I do feel a little peckish."

"Haha, funny! It's barbecued beef, of course. Is there even any other?"

"OK. I'll make some cheese and salad sandwiches

31

and eat with your grandmother."

"Fine. Oh no! I can't believe it! I nearly had my sword! Mum, the Internet is off again!"

"Can't you do something else then? Like read!"

"Come to the garden, darling. Tell me, what are you reading?"

"Oh, nothing, Granny. Mum's complaining because she wants me to read more. Actually, I found a really old book in the cupboard the other day. *Treasure Island*. Do you know it?"

"Oh, yes. That was James' favourite. It's an adventure at sea – about a search for buried treasure – by a young boy, Jim, and some ruthless pirates who start a mutiny."

"What's a mutiny?"

"Like a rebellion, a riot."

"Sounds good. I might give it a go. At least it'll keep Mum off my back."

"I'm sure you'll find it interesting, dear."

"Yes… er, no offence, Gran, but your Internet sucks."

"Sucks? Whatever are you talking about, child?"

"Oh, doesn't matter. Love you."

"Bless you. I love you too."

***

"Got the pizza. Come in now, Joe, needs to be eaten before it gets cold. Are you and Mary sorted for food, love? I knew you wouldn't want any of this, so I didn't ask."

"Yes, don't worry. We're fine. Come and sit down in

your chair, Mum. I'll plump the cushions up for you. I've brushed the dog fur off."

"Thanks, darling. I do love this chair. Mum said Granny bought it before my Uncle Danny went to war. You *will* keep it when I die, won't you? It's part of the family and holds a special place in my heart."

"Please don't talk about dying. Of course we'll keep it, Mum."

"That's good to hear. You know, when I was a child, I played 'Cops and Robbers' with James – he tied me to it and I fell, and the chair... well, never mind now. It's still so sturdy, given all the traffic it's endured over the many years – must be a hundred or more. But let me sit down. Rest my legs. Where are my slippers?"

"Maxi, let go of Granny's slippers this instant! How many times have I told you! Here you are, Mum, not too chewed. That dog is incorrigible! I'll put the fire on for you."

"Thank you, love."

And dear Mary, with silver-grey hair and pale-blue eyes like a calm autumn ocean, slowly lowers her fragile frame into my outstretched arms, and I strive to embrace, to soothe, to remain close by. Always.

For all generations who come my way – life goes on, and children play.

A FRESH START

He was a *yes* man, her husband. *Yes* to romantic weekends by the sea, *yes* to trying oysters, *yes* to buying a dog, but unfortunately, *yes* too to the brassy, loud-mouthed Trina with the huge cleavage and eternal pout who lived down the road. Naturally, the final *yes* was a *no* and his wife left him.

After hurling his brightly suggestive shirts, colourful socks adorned with symbols of Superman – *really?!* – and original *Private Eye* magazines out of the greedy-mouthed window, Juli stormed like hurricane Irene into the thus-far peaceful garden and, after yanking the rusty blunt shears from their two-year-long siesta in a cobwebby corner of the garage, viciously attacked the terrified hedge (which had not featured remotely in her husband's affair) with a frenzied, indeed violent, passion, clutching the still-sleepy weapon in her tightly clenched red fists.

"Bastard!" she screamed, scaring away any nearby birds and spraying the rapidly retreating cat with spittle. "I hate you! Bastard!"

When a few hours had passed, her now-tamed anger turned to tears and she sobbed fiercely while devouring chocolates and drinking pink gin in the company of dreadful romcoms and the poodle, Powderpuff.

"Bloody stupid name he chose for you! Ridiculous!"

And the dog (again not complicit in the shameful affair) briefly looked at her with wide, uncomprehending eyes before sadly retreating to the sanctuary of his basket.

The following week, friends – only those sympathetic to her predicament – had been invited to a party which lasted the entire night. Here, emotions, largely hers, were vented via frenzied dance, an abundant flow of alcohol and disparaging slurred talk of her ex, until morning shone a bright light on the battlefield of bottles, broken baguettes, cheese, olive sticks and crisps. And after the evening of much-needed therapy, she took an icy-cold shower to wash the man forever out of her hair, before moving on with a vengeance.

That was last year.

Since then, Juli had decided to relocate to a small village on the banks of the estuary. She had sold her house with ease and had embarked on a new adventure – a clean break. Away from her ex, away from any reminder of her past. A fresh start. Another life.

A cottage, just a stone's throw from the sea, had been purchased with tiny, blue-rimmed windows, whitewashed walls and a compact, grassed garden dotted with daisies and bordered with multicoloured cosmos and sweet william. Perfect. A veritable picture postcard.

And close by stood the popular local pub with its thatched roof and wooden beams – a hive of activity at the weekends; and adorning its walls hung an eclectic, almost Daliesque, array of clocks, of all shapes, sizes, colours, rendering this establishment her favourite haunt for a home-brewed beer and a book.

And the tick tock, tick tock of the clocks, tick tock, tick tock... cuckoo, resembled the mating call of an exotic bird, and entranced by this comforting beat, Juli relaxed into the cushioned leather chair and sipped the froth from her real ale. So nice here. So calm.

Over in the corner sat an old man with wiry silver hair, a weathered countenance and a lazy eye. No doubt he had some stories to tell, she mused.

Jim was his name and he had been a fisherman for over forty-five years, still owning his now paint-peeled fishing boat, which these days also enjoyed retirement and was mostly anchored in the pebbly cove, when not accommodating the occasional ferry ride to the neighbouring seaside for the spattering of summer tourists or 'grockles' as they were referred to in dialect.

He still wore his treasured waxy oilskin sou'wester reminiscent of former seafaring days. And his tipple was cider – several pints a night, before he swayed unsteadily home to his humble house, which happily hugged the bay.

Several other locals would spill into the pub daily, such as Miss Turnpike of the Women's Institute – poker-faced until she got to know you. And a neat doughnut bun with no give had been planted on her head since 1975, steadfastly secured by black grips.

Then there was Karl, the young boy from the fish trade, whose long, straw-blond hair, which he flicked back incessantly, harboured the distinct smell of clams;

and his girlfriend, Mandy – slender, fresh-faced, rosy-cheeked, from the newly emerged boutique on the corner of the main road – who seemed oblivious to this fishy perfume, given her constant canoodling.

Another frequent visitor to the pub was Greg – to his face and 'Grumps' in his absence – and his special chair by the window was sacrosanct, which Juli had soon learned.

"That's my chair you're sitting in, young lady. My chair! Now be so good as to move!" the stocky, red-faced farmer had stated emphatically. And being the newcomer, she had not wished to offend and briskly jumped up like a jack-in-the-box, instinctively brushing the plump velvet cushion with her hand before promptly transferring to a diminutive seat by the bar.

"Don't worry about him, love," said the bartender with a smile. "His bark's worse than his bite. He used to be a sergeant major in the army. I pity his wife, so I do! Are you here to stay then?"

"That's the plan. It's so peaceful. I love the smell of fresh, salty sea air and the relaxed pace. My name's Juli, by the way. Pleased to meet you."

"Bill," said the man. "Likewise. Welcome to Seastone. Your dog will be in his element here. Plenty of open spaces. What's he called?"

"Powi," she replied. And even though acute confusion had resided on poor Powderpuff's face for several weeks following this change, he had finally managed to learn his new name, now proudly embracing this simple, yet punchy, little word and finding his current identity rather appealing.

The church bell struck twelve in the village square, scaring the bats in the belfry, as Saturday finally gave way to Sunday. On the ultimate chime, Juli, starved of sleep, had ventured downstairs and watched a chilling thriller, probably not the best choice for insomnia, which had left her even more wide awake and somewhat apprehensive too.

A glass of wine had been poured before she opened her front door to breathe in some much-needed fresh air and also to observe the moon brush its luminescent silver light over the dark sea.

"How beautiful," she admired.

Lowering herself onto the functional wooden chair, which must have lived outside for decades given its warped seat, she placed her wine glass on its faithful companion, a tiny, shabby chic – leaning more towards shabby – round table. Her favourite turquoise and pink flecked shawl, bought in the local market, was wrapped around her shoulders as the air was chilly.

It was shortly after this that a barely audible knock could be heard from nearby, followed by a loud whisper: "Jim, I'm here. Open up quick." The ex-fisherman lived at the bottom of the lane, which was now lit only by a dim streetlamp.

Curiosity getting the better of her, Juli inched forward to further explore this sound which broke the silence and was shocked to glimpse a familiar figure, a semi-silhouette eagerly awaiting access to Jim's house. That tightly pinned bun, like a meticulously constructed birds' nest, was instantly recognisable anywhere, and this unexpected sight had her staring in disbelief.

It was not long before the door creaked ajar, and the woman vanished from view.

"You dark horse, Miss Turnpike. Who would have thought it!" And these whispered words dissolved secretively into the all-knowing, all-seeing night.

She really couldn't imagine Miss Turnpike ever having a man! It was hard to conceive of her actually touching another human being with platonic affection, let alone intimacy. But maybe peachy lace underwear lurked seductively under that high-waisted tweed skirt and knitted cardigan, and not a reinforced bra and stays as one would have expected. And she chuckled to herself.

Early morning came and Juli, who, despite her sleepless night, was up with the larks, placed her milk bottle out just in time to catch the furtive femme fatale stealthily emerging into the still-drowsy dawn. But the bottle teetered and fell, and Miss Turnpike followed the clatter with her alert eyes only to observe the smiling girl looking directly at her from the porch.

"Good morning, Miss Turnpike," she grinned.

Mortified, the woman, bun dishevelled and flat, like a trodden-on scone, and grips awry, bade a hasty good day before disappearing round the corner with amazing velocity for someone of her years – she was no spring chicken.

That evening, as Juli entered the pub, Miss Turnpike's usually pale face transformed to a bright scarlet as she caught the girl's eye, and she shuffled uncomfortably in her chair.

"How are you?" asked Juli.

"Oh, er fine," she replied, firmly gripping her sherry glass. "I just popped round to Jim's this morning to deliver some milk as he said he'd run out."

"Of course," returned Juli. "Very neighbourly of you."

"He likes a cup of tea in the morning."

Yes, and I wonder what he likes at night! But naturally, these words were not voiced out loud.

Bill, who had overheard this discourse, grinned as Juli approached the bar.

"Taking milk to Jim again, was she? He seems to run out several times a week." And he winked.

"You know?"

"The whole village knows, love. You'd think she'd vary her story after all these years!"

Two weeks later, as the forecast seemed promising, Juli decided to pack a picnic, hire a boat and row to a nearby bay. And as he glimpsed the red-check linen cloth in the wicker basket, Powi barked with excitement; this undoubtedly meant an outdoor trip with treats.

"Come on. Let's go, while it's so warm!" she beckoned, and the duo made for the shore.

Bright rays of sunshine kissed the calm sea as girl and dog hit the waters, both charged with avid enthusiasm nurtured by the warm day and imminent adventure. The secluded bay could be reached in just under an hour, but after a while rowing, Juli's arms ached acutely, and a brief pause was required.

"I don't think I've worked these muscles so much in years. They're not used to hard graft."

"Woof, woof," came her companion's animated, yet patient, reply as he waited for the journey to recommence.

Eventually, their destination was reached and the boat tied securely to a rock. A pleasant spot on the sandy beach was selected, sheltered by the surrounding white cliffs, and the picnic devoured with overwhelming gusto, ravenous hound effortlessly polishing off every last morsel.

Exhausted, Juli dozed, while Powi bounced like a kangaroo round the bay, leaping in and out of rock pools, gazing fascinated at a tantalising crab sidling by, which he yearned to play with but dared not touch – he had never met such a creature before, all shell and pincers, like a spider in armour! Maybe it was aware of his attention as it soon slid into the water, seeking refuge under a small rock. So, instead, the dog busied himself with a clump of wet sea lettuce, which had drifted to shore.

"Come on, Powi! Here boy!" called Juli, a good hour later. "Let's go for a swim!" And she raced, like an eager child, full of anticipation, to the inviting waters.

Promptly abandoning his last plaything – a seagull's feather, the dog bounded excitedly into the sparkling sea, creating a fountain of spray, which churned the resident fish into a fearful frenzy.

"Wonderful all of this," Juli sighed. "Just wonderful!"

But unfortunately, these famous last words were short-lived. Towards late afternoon, waves gradually appeared from nowhere, surging forth with an unsettling certainty, and the girl's tranquil mood turned to one of angst.

"We need to get out of here – this doesn't feel right!" And her fear was mirrored by Powi, who twitched nervously while awaiting further instructions.

Belongings were hurriedly gathered, and the empty picnic basket swept up like lightning. The fragile boat rocked unsteadily to and fro. It seemed much smaller now than it had earlier on, she thought, as she untethered it with shaking hands and clambered aboard, dog just a split second behind.

Using all the force she could muster, she prised it from the rock with her oars, until only foamy white water was left surrounding the now-quaking vessel. Remaining in the bay hadn't been an option as, by evening, the tide would carry the sea right up to the cliffs, leaving this the only possible exit.

Progress was deadly slow, the slender oars feeble in their fight against the increasingly choppy sea. And sucking at the tiny, wooden craft, the bullying breakers rose remorselessly, ready to swallow both boat and vulnerable victims in their vast and frothing mouths. Juli determined to focus solely on the moment while attempting, at all costs, to deliver them both home alive.

"It's OK, Powi, don't worry," she said in a voice tinged with dread. And he sat shaking in a small space at the bottom of their watery cell.

It was not long into the arduous voyage before the boat teetered on the brink, scarcely able to keep afloat against this fierce foe of foam. And these terrible moments lingered until, towering out of the blue, a monstrous wave, as high as a mountain, loomed. Juli shuddered inadvertently and let out a shriek.

"Keep down!" she screamed, causing the dog to exude a terrified howl. Their imminent fate was no longer in her hands. Only God could save them now.

The powerful breaker advanced with lightning speed until it landed with a ferocious crash just inches away, thus hurling Powi into the waiting waves, before completely overturning the frail vessel. Instinctively, Juli grabbed the ropes, clinging on for dear life, and heaved herself onto the capsized wooden skiff where she lay, screaming helplessly into the deep, dark depths.

"Powi, Powi! Come back! Powi! My darling Powderpuff!" But all to no avail. Her cries were met with a terrible silence.

After what seemed an eternity, with hands chafed from her ever-tightening grip on the cord, Juli was conscious of dusk descending and became gravely aware that if she failed to act now, she would surely die. She needed to roll the boat over; this would be her only chance. So, heaving and heaving with a Goliath-like might, after several failed attempts, she finally managed to turn the flimsy vessel right-side up and tumbled gratefully into its fragile lap. "Thank God!" she cried as she lay shivering unremittingly, devastated for poor Powi, miserably awaiting her fate. And she sobbed silently into the uncaring night.

Little did she know that, due to rough waters, Karl was returning earlier than usual with his abundant catch.

"We'll get to shore just in time, I reckon," he called out.

"Yeah, 'cause weather'll get worse afore it gets better," shouted Jo, his long-time friend and business partner.

"Did great with the fishing today though, mate."

"Yeah. Good catch, better'n last week."

"Wait! Did you hear something?"

"No. What?"

"Like a bark, a faint bark… listen. Shine the torch."
And they both peered over the side of the boat.

"Over there. Look."

And forlornly clutching onto some floating flotsam, like an aged limpet to a rock, dangerously close to losing his battle against the elements, was the wretched, bedraggled dog, his feeble bark resounding in terror.

"Quick! Chuck in the lifebuoy! Check the rope's attached!" shouted Karl.

"Yeah, 's all good!" And, without further ado, Jo tossed the buoy overboard with expert precision. "Here boy, here. Hold on! Come on boy, you'll be OK. Come on!"

And the miserable creature, sensing a fragment of hope, paddled frantically forward until its exhausted limbs reached out and gripped onto the side of the lifebuoy with a fearful force.

"Atta boy. Hold on, hold on tight!" And crying out words of encouragement, they dragged the shivering passenger closer and closer to safety.

"Last lap now. Cling on, boy, cling on!" And a deft heave had them easing buoy and dog out of the water and into the waiting boat.

"Oh my God, it's Powi!" exclaimed Karl, tenderly cradling the traumatised animal in his arms. "Powi! – Wait, so if Powi's here, where's Juli? Where the hell is Juli? She must be in danger too."

And, to confirm these fears, the dog, albeit weak, leapt out of the boy's gentle grasp and bounded with a frightful urgency to the edge of the boat, barking incessantly into the night. Fully comprehending, Karl and Jo circled the waters near the bay, shouting out Juli's name at the tops of their voices, over the roaring waves. But nothing. Again, they circled, torch shining brightly onto the pitch-black seas. Until, eventually, the form of a tiny, drowning vessel could be detected, bobbing hysterically up and down.

"That's it! That's it! Slow up, let's get a better look." And, at the sea-soaked bottom of the battered, slowly sinking boat, there lay the girl, limp like a ragdoll.

"Juli!" they shouted. "Juli!" But no response.

The waves were high… huge, growing more forceful by the second.

"We have to act fast, or it will be too late," stressed Karl, seizing his life jacket and saftey rope.

"It's too dangerous, mate."

"No, I'll be fine. We don't have much time." And, without procrastination, he threw on the jacket.

"Now, lower me down and shine the torch."

Not wanting to argue, and sensing there might just be a chance, Jo lowered his friend over the side.

"Shine the torch!"

"OK, mate, good luck! You can jump now!" And Karl plunged into the treacherous waters.

"Juli!" he cried out. "Juli!" But the menacing waves engulfed him, dragging him under with a terrible force; and copious amounts of the salty liquid left him coughing and spluttering, as he bounced, with grim resolve, back up to the surface and swam vigorously towards the light. But too late, the boat had been buffeted mercilessly away.

"It's not here," he yelled in desperation. "It's shifted! Shine it over to the right!"

"What?" cried Jo.

"To the right!" he repeated frantically.

"OK!"

It was then that the sorry little boat came into view and in minutes he had reached it and was clinging firmly to the edge. Losing no time, he cautiously clambered in, pulling the limp body towards him. A faint groan could be heard, followed by a low, rasping sound, and this filled him with hope.

"Juli, stay with me now. It's going to be fine, just stay with me."

And, swiftly, he tugged the rope twice and raised his arm. The spotlight, now clipped fixedly to its stand, shone directly on them, as Jo hauled the helpless skiff resolutely back to base.

"Throw down the ladder! Quick!" entreated Karl. And enfolding Juli securely in his grasp, he heaved them both onto the lowest rung. The waves boxed the side of the sturdy vessel over and over with increasing ferocity, but his firm grip on the rope ladder, which flapped back and forth like a captured bird, was unflagging. It was crucial to remain calm at this critical point and he knew only too well that correct timing would mean the difference between life and death.

A moment later, Juli started to come round and, panic-stricken, wrestled to break free, until she understood where she was. In seconds, Karl lost his footing, and the pair were thrust off balance, but with the dexterity and speed of a seasoned mamba, he lunged forwards unflinching, grabbing the edge of the last rung.

"All good, mate?" shouted Jo, his voice fraught with anxiety.

"Yeah! Coming up!" And he clambered onto the next and then the next foothold until they were halfway up.

"Two more rungs and I can reach you! Keep going!"

The waves struck incessantly, and his ascent was laboured, but he remained steadfast, resolute.

"Nearly there, Juli, nearly there. Hold on tight," he reassured. And soon Jo was able to ease her over the edge to safety, with Karl supporting from behind.

And Powi, his sheer joy at beholding Juli immeasurable, could scarcely contain himself; he licked her face in adoration, like his favourite peanut butter treat, wildly wagging his animated tail, and she embraced her beloved dog with such fervour that he could scarcely catch his breath.

The story of their day gradually unfolded, and Karl and Jo were thanked avidly for their brave rescue. Within a short while, the boat had been moored in the nearby harbour. And forthwith, Karl phoned Mandy, who arrived in minutes to drive Juli and Powi home.

"Let me make you a warm cup of tea," she offered, once inside. "And I'll run you a hot bath."

"Oh, wonderful," came the appreciative reply. "Thank you."

"You had a lucky escape, you know."

"Yes," agreed Juli soberly. "Very lucky. Karl was so brave. We owe our lives to him."

And Mandy smiled proudly.

The next day, there was a loud knock at the door, and Juli was surprised to see Greg with a huge bouquet of flowers.

"A gift for you, my dear," he explained in a surprisingly shy voice. "You gave us all a scare, you know. Everyone is so relieved you're back safely. And Miss Turnpike will be visiting later with a home-made cake."

"How kind. Thank you. The flowers are beautiful."

"I wanted to tell you that myself and the good lady will be attending a wedding in Somerset, and we'll be away for a week. So, you're welcome to sit in my chair when you're down the pub."

"Oh, that's sweet of you. Thanks," came her response. "Have a wonderful time."

"Right then, goodbye," he replied, awkwardly taking his leave.

"Wow, have his chair for a whole week! You are most definitely one of the favoured few," grinned Bill that evening.

And no sooner had she sat down, savouring the luxury of this cushioned throne, than she glimpsed a young man enter the lounge, with rugged features, curly black hair and large wellingtons (who said wellingtons weren't sexy!), and her eyes followed him as he sauntered casually to the other end of the bar... alone. She smiled contentedly to herself. "Maybe," she mused, as she sipped her real ale. "Who knows!"

AN
UNDERSTANDING

A quiet, insular boy, with fine, silk-brown hair, gentle eyes and a shy yet engaging smile: this was Matthew. Content to play on his bike, read Marvel comics and watch *Doctor Who*. An only child and the apple of his mother's eye. His stammer, partly genetic, worsened with anxiety. His father had stammered severely as a child, but in adulthood his impediment had become less pronounced. Mother had taken Matty (as she called him) to a therapist, who had patiently guided him through a multitude of exercises to improve vocal flow, some of which had helped, some not.

During registration, the teacher, briefly glancing up at his chair, had started placing a tick by his name without requesting a response. This practice had been implemented to avoid his struggle with the words 'present, Miss' which initiated, on a daily basis, a low echo of 'p-p-p' and 'm-m-m' to resound in the room, despite her constant chastisement of the cruel offenders. Clearly, no inkling was had that this kindly intended gesture had induced the poor boy to feel as if he were somehow invisible, but not in a good way like Sue Storm from his Marvel comics, instead with a stark sense of deficiency.

When alone, tranquillity reigned, so naturally the boy relished his own company, rather than that of other children, who giggled, guffawed, jested and mimicked when they witnessed his broken, laboured utterances. But sadly, the playground could not often be avoided.

"Oh look, it's M-M-M-Matthew. H-H-Hi." Tommy was the worst of them. A stocky boy, far taller than the others. Always had bruises on his arms and legs. Funny that, mused Matthew, Tommy was surely a predator, not a victim; only yesterday he had pulled little Molly's hair so hard that a sizeable clump had been forced to detach itself from her tender scalp. The pain had left her screaming like a lynx, until a formidable teacher on playground duty had come bounding to her rescue. For the rest of the day, the boy had been confined to a small, grey room adjoining the head's office, until his parents, who had been summoned, had arrived for a *chat* regarding his unacceptable behaviour.

The following day, and the next, saw his chair empty, and when he eventually surfaced, yet more bruises – many more, like blemished fruit or shoddy tattoos – had angrily invaded his arms and legs, furnishing him with renewed venom.

"G-G-Get over h-h-here, l-l-loser!" he had bawled once beyond the school gates. And Matthew, desperately considering his shrunken options, had decided that, in truth, there were scarce any, except maybe to flee; but given that Tommy could outrun him any day, he had been forced to reluctantly face his aggressor, only to receive a fierce blow to the head, sending him reeling across the path and into a needly gorse, which had pricked his slight frame with piercing intensity, adding to his already mounting agony. So, yes, understandably, playing alone was much favoured by the child, who inevitably sought to dodge his peers, especially Tommy, at all costs, which meant concealing himself behind walls or bushes, even up a tree once, until his tormentors had well and truly departed.

On this aforementioned day, Matty had arrived home, head throbbing, ripped clothes covered in mud.

"Oh my God! What on earth has happened to you?" exclaimed his mother, acute angst wrinkling her hitherto calm complexion.

"I-I-It's n-nothing." And the traumatised child burst into tears.

"Well, it most certainly doesn't look like nothing to me!" she asserted but, suddenly aware of her son's pitiful state, softened her tone. "Come here, darling. It'll be OK; trust me." And she gently hugged the shaking boy.

"I f-f-fell in a b-bush, th-that's all," he said in a whisper, arms dangling limply by his side.

"Bushes don't punch you in the head, darling, now, do they. Tell me the truth," she persisted.

"I-If I t-tell you th-the truth, m-m-my life w-won't be worth l-living, Mum."

"Look, we can't let whoever did this go unpunished! They should suffer the consequences. We need to act right away. Is it anyone you know? Someone from school?"

There was a long pause before the reluctant response. "Y-yes."

"Who?"

"W-will you p-promise not t-to say anyth-thing if I t-tell you?"

"I can't do that, sweetheart. It's best for everyone that we expose the culprit – we can't just accept this violation."

"T…" he muttered after a while.

"Who?"

"T-T-T-Tommy."

"Tommy? Wait, I've heard that name before. Molly's mum – she said he attacked her daughter the other day. Yanked her hair out or something equally heinous."

"Y-yes… and he keeps m-making fun of m-my stutter. Every d-day he w-waits for me and t-taunts me in f-front of the other ki-kids," he gushed, now eagerly releasing his previously tethered torment.

"Right, that's it." And an angry visit to the school had ensued. This time, however, following a heated debate, the bully had been suspended.

"He should have been expelled!" protested Mother, crossing her arms irately.

"Suspension just isn't enough for the likes of him – for a vile bully. Society's gone soft," she grumbled to her husband later that evening.

"At least… at least it's something positive," he had replied calmly, and the matter was closed.

Monday, after school, saw Matthew wandering by the lakeside, earphones attached, singing along to his favourite tunes. This exercise had been highly recommended by his therapist, and he found that the words having to be voiced at an exact time aided him in controlling his stammer. And peace – indeed fun, was found in this escape.

Climbing down the hill to the bank, he recalled his mother's words –*Don't, whatever you do, go near the edge* – and he smiled. Taking off his shoes and socks, he tentatively dipped his toes, followed by both feet, into the icy water and gasped in pleasure at the sheer exhilaration of this simple activity. He gazed over the flowing expanse of shimmering silver gently reflecting the surrounding willows; it was then that he noticed a body on the far bank, curled up tight like a crumpled paper ball… and gently rocking. Gingerly, he crept along the water's edge and up into the bushes, gradually drawing nearer and nearer in order to observe with more clarity. His headphones were carefully placed into his rucksack so that all his senses were on full alert. And, listening now, he heard muffled crying carried by the soft breeze and saw a boy sitting on the bank, arms hugging his drawn-up knees, steadily rocking to and fro. And, all of a sudden it seemed, drawn by an invisible force, Matthew found himself just a few metres away.

A sleeping bag lay limply on the coarse grass, a water bottle by its side. And a packet of prawn cocktail crisps – a flavour, incidentally, that Matty detested.

After silent reflection, he spoke.

"H-Hi. Are you OK? W-Why are you crying?" he asked innocently.

Mortified at being discovered in such a vulnerable stance, the boy leapt up, like a cat on hot bricks, to view this unwelcome intruder. It was only then that Matthew became fully aware of the much, much larger form rising up, like a giant, right in front of him. And he shuddered. It was Tommy, who now stared at the terrified boy, a quiet fury residing in his red, puffy eyes.

"What are you doing here, loser! Did you follow me? Get away, while you still can! You tell anyone you saw me and you're dead. You understand, DEAD!" he screamed, reaching out to grab the rapidly retreating child, who now ran frantically in the direction of home.

And flying into the sanctuary of his front door, Matty flopped down into the reassuring comfort of his favourite armchair.

"Hi, darling. You're all out of breath. Are you alright?"

"Yes, I'm fine, Mum. D-Don't worry." And he disappeared to his room, ever thankful, and puzzled too, that Tommy had let him go.

So why, in Heaven's name, did he return the next morning? Curiosity? Sympathy? But he did. Two rounds of cheese and tomato sandwiches were wrapped and secreted in his rucksack, later accompanied by a six pack of prawn cocktail crisps bought from the local store en route to the lake. Not forgetting two bottles of water.

"OK. Here goes," he said under his breath.

Matty had never skipped school before, and he hoped his mother would not find out. If he forged a note for the following day, all should be fine. Fingers crossed.

As he approached the spot he had last encountered Tommy, trepidation took root. His shoulders ached and goosebumps, like grains of sand, sprouted on his arms and legs.

"He's j-just a b-boy, like me," he repeated soothingly to himself. "J-just a boy."

But when he emerged from behind the bushes and crept past the old willow tree to view the lakeside, Tommy was not there. Hesitantly, he searched the area but to no avail. And he was on the verge of leaving when he heard a cough drifting from the woodland to the west side of the lake. Drawn by the sound, he tiptoed towards it, soon coming across the shivering boy huddled up in a bed of fern under a tree. And he stood silently watching until Tommy sensed his presence and spun round.

"What the hell are you doing here?! Got a death wish or something, loser!"

"I-I'm n-not a l-loser," came the simple response. "I'm a st-st... I stutter. And I-I'm n-not scared of you. Not anymore," he added. "Y-You're just a b-boy, like me. And I w-want to help you."

"Help me! *You* help *me*! Are you mad! I should kick your arse!"

"I-I've brought some f-food. Are you hungry?" asked Matty, ignoring the threat.

Without a word, Tommy snatched the sandwiches and devoured them ravenously.

"How did you know I like prawn cocktail crisps?" he said, ripping open the bag.

"I saw a p-packet on the g-grass yesterday. They're d-disgusting."

There was a pause, before Tommy relaxed his shoulders ever so slightly, inadvertently mirroring Matty's gentle smile.

"I've run away," he confided shortly. "Got nowhere else to go, so I stay here."

"I'll b-bring my d-dog tomorrow," replied Matty, unsure of what to say. "He's a L-Labrador, his name's L-Lotty. And I'll g-get more food."

"Can you bring a coat? It's bloody freezing at night-time."

"Aren't you sc-scared, out here alone when it's d-dark?"

"I'm not scared of anything! Not even my dad!" And he trembled.

"I m-missed school to c-come here."

"Wait. So you're a badass now?"

"M-Maybe." And Matty giggled.

"Thanks, by the way, for the food... and sorry."

"S-Sorry?"

"For before..." replied Tommy. "I... I..." The boy struggled with probably his first ever attempt at a genuine apology.

"Haha, y-you've c-caught my st-stutter," smiled Matthew, inviting a wide grin to spread like butter over Tommy's lips.

"Remember to bring a coat," the boy urged before long.

"I'll try. S-See you." And, with a new-found spring in his step, Matty left.

However, on returning the next afternoon with Lotty, who charged relentlessly in and out of the feathery reeds, splashing the ice-cold water into a geyser-like spray, Matthew, despite a lengthy search, could not find a single trace of the boy. Nothing. So he slipped off his shoes and socks and dipped his feet in the water, much to the delight of his eager hound. And he felt different now. Stronger somehow.

The following day, he waited purposefully at the teacher's desk until she arrived.

"I-I w-want t-to answer my name when you call the register, l-like the others," he requested.

"Of course, Matthew," came the reply. "If you're sure."

But this time, when the boy's name was called, each classmate, sensing his determination, waited patiently for him to finish. And their silence empowered him.

And a few weeks later, when Tommy returned to school, an aura of tranquillity filled the air. They had a secret connection now – an understanding. There was no longer a need to hide. All was calm.

THE GALLERY
OF DREAMS

Photos of paintings by Henry Scott Tuke (1858–1929)
and Claude Monet (1840–1926).

O ften, he would find himself here in the Gallery of Dreams. In fact, most days really. Despite the discomfort of the cold, marble bench, he would seek solace in the high-ceilinged airy hall where he could be lured effortlessly into other worlds.

One particular painting left him spellbound, mesmerised, and he lost himself in what might be, rather than what was. Such pure yet sensual images, accentuated by the sparkling allure of the sea... sun-stroked water on skin... the innocence, vulnerability, rendered him sane and warm, in stark contrast to the bleak black-and-white world in which he lived. These sculpted, highlighted bodies, young, golden, relaxed... chatting, lounging, looking... living, gave him hope. Here was an endearing simplicity – no need to hide or pretend. With the delicate, glassy droplets glistening over the sun-kissed forms, came the embodiment of beauty, of verve, and he felt alive in this presence.

To merge into the painting was his desire. To be an active part of this sublime tableau, this perfection. But where would he place himself? Beside the youths on the sand – or with the child in the sea? The boys on the bank, where did their thoughts lie... what secret dialogue did they impart to each other? Did they criticise or applaud the youth in the sea for his unbridled joy? Oh, how he longed to know! To blend in, to be a part of this idyllic scene, this utopia! So estranged from his own mundane existence, his wooden world, his incarceration.

***

The far end of the high-ceilinged hall saw an old lady settled on a padded wooden chair. Rising at dawn, she had eaten her solitary breakfast, accompanied by a strong cup of tea, before strolling across the pigeon-cluttered square to sit staring at a young woman and child in her favourite painting.

The tiny, yet welcoming, cottage at the top of the hill was where she imagined herself, as a maid maybe or an old aunt, grandmother even.

The young woman, blue parasol in hand like a sail, and lace-layered dress brushing lightly against the delicate flowers, swept down the poppy-coated field with carefree abandon – a possible granddaughter perhaps? She would call her Charlotte. And the small child? Alfred, yes, that would suit well. Donning a summer straw boater and clutching a posy of ruddy poppies, he seemed such a happy boy. How she would love to hold his little hand!

The open countryside, caressed, no doubt, by a fresh, mild breeze, beckoned the aged woman and she breathed in this heavenly calm, this Eden of perfection, causing her gnawing loneliness to temporarily dissolve.

The blissful scene brought tears to her eyes – the young woman and her zest for life, the cheery child, untroubled, free. And who was the girl on top of the hill? Who could she be? Charlotte's sister, friend – Amy? Yes, Amy. And her child must surely be Annie. Oh, how she yearned to be with them, to receive their laughter and live in this serene world, so alien from her own dingy room with hard, ungiving surfaces, frugal decor and sad net curtains drawn over the small windows like filmy cataracts, shadowing the world outside.

***

Just a week later, as he sat fully immersed in the painting, a boy about his age appeared on the marble bench beside him and said:

"It's funny, at first glance they seem so relaxed and carefree, but when you look closer, you notice a certain awkwardness in their demeanour, as if self-confidence is an aspect they are still inwardly striving to achieve, rather than one they have already mastered." He smiled. "At least, that's how it appears to me. My name's Jules by the way. Pleased to meet you."

"Andre," came the thoughtful reply. "You could be right; I hadn't considered that." And he savoured the soft voice, intense eyes and delighted in the dishevelled dark-blond locks.

Their animated discussion on this and many other occasions was honest and impassioned, resulting in numerous visits to the gallery, nearby coffee shop and a meal out in a rustic restaurant, where a warm orange candle cast a cosy glow over the table, further illuminating their expectant faces. And now his shoulders felt light, relaxed, not heavy and aching as before, and there was laughter in his eyes, which his sister had noticed.

"You've found someone!"

"Yes," came the shy response.

"I knew it!" And she held him close.

And one afternoon, as he sat contentedly on the comfortably cool marble bench, holding Jules' hand and admiring the picture they never tired of (which had prompted an enchanting trip to sunny Cornwall), he wondered what the boys on the sand would see if they turned around. For now, Andre belonged in his own vivid canvas, and he basked in the colourful splendour of his heavenly bond… a veritable tableau of perfection.

***

The very next morning, the old lady decided to prepare a picnic to share with whom she now firmly believed were her new family.

And, sauntering into the gallery, ignoring the 'No Food' sign, she settled happily on her chair.

"I've got egg and cress for you, Charlotte," she explained. "And honey for Alfred and Annie. Amy has prawn. What a beautiful day it is, with such an embracing breeze. I'm delighted to be here with you all. Give me a hug, my dears."

Noticing the elderly woman with arms outstretched and sandwich in hand, the receptionist neared, asking if all were fine while gently chastising her for paying no attention to the rules of the establishment.

"Madam, may I remind you there is a no eating policy in the gallery."

"But I'm having a picnic with my family," came the happy reply. "Who are you?"

Understanding now, that she must adopt a slightly more flexible approach to cater for this frail and somewhat confused individual, the receptionist kindly added, "OK, on this one occasion, I will overlook the situation, but please do not be too long and ensure you put your rubbish in the bin when you have finished."

"Of course, I shall," came the emphatic response. "I do know the countryside must be respected at all times."

That evening, she had to admit, the walk up the hill to her cottage had been a bit of a struggle – she was no spritely youth anymore, but what a lovely day she had had.

It was nigh on a week later when the unobservant milkman finally noticed her milk had not been collected. And when neighbours forced open her door, the old lady was found in a wooden rocking chair, picnic basket by her side and the traces of a smile still lingering on her silver lips.

MAN AND CAT

"Welcome, Mr. Dory. I hope you'll be very happy here. These are the keys to your new cottage."

After his wife's death, Sam had been told by friends that the country air would do him good, help him heal, but no one understood that he was long dead, just a shadow of the man he had once been when Cassie was there. Now he had no energy, no purpose, no reason. After three years, the rawness of the pain he had suffered before had slipped into numbness, which sometimes gave way to intense grief when a triggered memory cruelly sucked him into the past; so he strove not to think about times gone by – about her. During the day, mundane yet necessary tasks were performed, such as chopping logs for the fire to keep warm and cooking food to stay alive, if that were the right word, given his frame of mind. And in the evening, he would read and drink vodka until he sank into a fitful sleep.

The village was a fair trek down muddy, spindly tracks to a spiralling road puckered with potholes, and then straight on, until the church, a smattering of small shops and a public house came into view.

"Hello, Mr. Dory. The oranges are nice and juicy

today and the fish caught just an hour since," greeted Maude, the friendly shopkeeper.

"OK, thanks." And he picked up the essentials – fish, milk, bread, vodka, and made for the till. Never did he engage in any form of dialogue save the bare minimum.

"Funny man, not very chatty, a little stand-offish," remarked Doreen from down the hill when he had left.

"He lost his wife several years ago and is a bit of a hermit by all accounts," replied Maude.

"His hair needs a comb through it. And his trousers look like they've never seen an iron."

"Well, he's clearly depressed and doesn't care about his attire."

"I noticed he bought vodka. That's not a good sign. Do you think he's an alcoholic?" persisted Doreen.

"I'm sure I don't know, but it isn't our business," replied the shopkeeper firmly. "That'll be twenty pounds, please."

"Well, he looks a bit shifty to me. I wouldn't trust *him* on a dark night. Twenty pounds! Everything's so expensive these days, but I don't suppose it's your fault. Bye now," she said before disappearing through the door to continue her gossip with anyone who had ears. And Maude sighed.

An ornamental urn containing Cassie's ashes, had, soon after Sam's arrival, been stored securely in the depths of a solid-oak sideboard, as being on display had rendered them a constant reminder of her death. A severe heart attack had stolen her from him. It had appeared out of nowhere and callously consumed her life in just thirty minutes, five minutes before help had finally arrived.

"Don't go down that road over again," he chastised himself. "No point in dwelling on the past. It's done now and there's no changing it." And, listlessly, he picked up his cap, pulled on his threadbare woollen coat and trundled outside to put on his wellingtons. "Should have got a size smaller," he sighed. "Cassie would've known. Never mind now."

One step in front of the other, he trudged mechanically down the track and over the stile, vacantly traversing the field until he arrived at the river's edge. The deep-blue flowers dotted along the bank passed by unnoticed as he traipsed onwards.

A few miles upstream, however, as he gazed over the reed-knotted water, a torn black bin liner semi-submerged in the shallows drew his attention. He had not expressed curiosity in anything since Cassie's passing, but now he found himself gingerly stepping amidst shiny wet stones, painstakingly plodding in the ill-fitting wellingtons across the width of the river until the partially bloated bag was in close range. After tentatively squeezing it and finding it both hard, yet soft, he hauled it out of the water, yanking it over his shoulders like a sack of potatoes, before lumbering back to shore. Then laying it on the bank, he unknotted the rough rope which was tied tightly around the neck of the sack, like a noose, and peeped warily inside.

"Jesus!" he cried, jumping back in shock. "Who could do such a thing!"

Quickly collecting himself, he carefully lifted out four tiny, soaking kittens, their soggy fur sticking fast to limp, cold corpses, terror still visible on their little faces.

"I'm too late," he lamented, sadly recalling a line in a Heaney poem where Dan Taggart had referred to the kittens he ruthlessly drowned as 'scraggy wee shits.' And tears surfaced in Sam's eyes.

After tipping the rocks onto the ground, he placed the bag in his pocket to dispose of later. Then he sadly lay the lifeless cadavers under a flowering bush. But the exact moment he made to leave, a sound – a weak sound, very weak, but indubitably a sound – could be deciphered! Heart pounding, he reached out, gently lifting a small, shivering form into the womb of his arms, enfolding his scarf around its feeble, shaking frame before lightly stroking its tiny head. And tenderly holding his new charge, he followed the windy track back to the cottage.

Once home, warm milk was lovingly prepared, which he offered the sorry creature via a syringe from his medical kit, and within seconds its minute pink tongue appeared, gratefully licking the milky nectar.

Shortly afterwards, the old man lowered it onto a cushion by the hearth where it slept soundly. And he pulled up his armchair and rested by its side.

"Lucky, that's what I'll call you," he said the next morning as he held the baby kitten close. "Lucky, I like that." And the faint purr which ensued suggested Lucky did as well.

Three weeks later, Sam found himself adding a flea collar and cat food – fresh oranges too, to his regular shopping list.

"You've got a cat," remarked Maude. "How nice."

"Yes," came his answer. Yet on this occasion, he wound up relating the entire story of the rescue. And he smiled as he pictured the precious kitten in its warm basket at home. "I'd better get back," he added. "I don't want to leave her for too long."

"Of course, love, take care," beamed Maude, delighted by this new connection.

And Doreen, who now stood by the till and had heard every word – one would expect nothing less – commented: "What a nice man. Didn't I tell you. I always knew it," before scuttling off to inform her neighbours of the latest developments.

"Unbelievable!" exclaimed Maude.

That afternoon, as Sam fondly ruffled the little cat's fur, his thoughts turned to Cassie, and this time, rather than sweeping them away, as was his wont, he allowed them to stay, embraced them even.

His wife had adored animals, and on one occasion when a stray dog had appeared on their doorstep, cold and starving, after bravely escaping a fierce and negligent owner, she had readily adopted him and, given they had no children, the dog had soon become an integral part of the family.

Many walks together across the heath were enjoyed, with dog meandering erratically through the purple heather and coarse green grasses, savouring the freedom of fresh air and vast, open spaces, and his presence had further enhanced their existing happiness.

"Cassie would have loved you," he said to Lucky. "And spoiled you rotten, that's for sure." And the cat, curled up contentedly like a ball of wool, gratefully received these pleasant words.

It was shortly after this that the old man leapt like a frenzied frog from his chair, causing Lucky, in a ripple reaction, to instinctively twitch.

"I know! Let's have a picnic!" he exclaimed, fondly remembering al fresco lunches in the shade of a pale-pink cherry blossom, which swept softly against the shrubs. "Cassie said it reminded her of candyfloss and marshmallows," he chuckled, dewy-eyed.

An orange seersucker cloth was folded and tuna sandwiches prepared before he made his way outside, cat, eagerly sniffing the fishy air, close behind.

The sun highlighted the pair as Sam reminisced, his weathered face lighting up like a child's as he related precious stories to the attentive, if bewildered, cat, who, after a sufficient period of patience, wondered if the tuna would ever come her way.

"We had a blackcurrant bush too. And Cassie made jam. I have never since tasted jam like hers – sharp yet sweet, with an enticingly fruity fragrance." And, at that moment, he had made his decision.

"That's it! I'll plant some blackcurrant bushes and make jam; I want to keep her memory alive in every way. But first," he added, "I'll buy a cherry blossom tree and scatter her ashes underneath."

And he sang that day; for the first time in three long years, he sang.

Lucky followed him everywhere, when she wasn't chasing butterflies or rodents, that is. On one occasion, she strode proudly up to the front door to present Sam with a gift: a playfully mauled mouse hanging helplessly from her dribbling jaws. But hastily bashing the poor victim's head with a stone to put it out of its misery, Sam had disposed of it in the neighbouring field. And Lucky, noting a certain lack of gratitude, had slumped off to sulk under the hedge.

Of late the sun had blessed so many days with its presence, and much time was spent outside, weeding unruly borders, planting summer flowers, tending the fragrant fruit, which, as well as blackcurrants, had now extended to juicy raspberries – gooseberries too. And Lucky, spread out like rolled marzipan on the daisied lawn, completed this Impressionist's dream.

"You'd be so pleased with the garden, Cassie," smiled Sam, proudly leaning on his sturdy spade. And a soothing rush of warmth flushed through him.

Later that afternoon, he strolled down the track, cautiously climbing over the splintery stile and into the field next to the riverbank. And he hummed softly as he ambled along, blissfully unaware of the squelchy fox muck directly ahead.

"Yuck!" he exclaimed as his sole left its squishy mark, like a wax seal, in the dung, and he hurriedly wiped his boot in a clump of long grass. Yet, suddenly, he found himself laughing out loud until he felt his sides splitting.

"Oh, Cassie, what a day that was," he grinned, recalling a walk in the country, where, caught off guard, he had lost his footing, tripped over a stone and landed less than gracefully in a freshly crafted cow pat. And she had roared with laughter, swiftly grabbing her camera from the rucksack so as to capture this hilarious spectacle.

"No, Cassie! What the hell! I'm covered in poo!"

"Don't be a baby, it's funny. Did you know that dogs roll around in fox poo, amongst other substances, because they find it empowering, and they believe the strong scent renders them attractive to other canines?"

"I'm not a bloody dog, though." He could not help but smile at her, however. She always seemed so very hopeful – a glass half-full person, which inevitably brought out the best in him.

"Maybe you want to be more attractive to me, darling, but you really needn't have gone to all this trouble," she jested. "I'm perfectly happy with you as you are."

"You find this a great joke, don't you! OK, come over here then."

And, fully understanding his intention, a high-pitched screech hit the air and she ran like a coyote across open land, with Sam in hot pursuit.

"No, don't you dare! *No!*" she yelled. But too late, he held her in his arms and kissed her.

And the river flowed peacefully by.

The following spring saw Sam sitting in the garden, with Lucky by his side nibbling on a chicken leg. He spread his home-made jam (not quite as tasty as Cassie's but good nevertheless) onto a clotted-cream scone and gazed at the soft, silky petals of the cherry blossom he had planted. These fragile blooms, their presence fleeting, served as a special remembrance, and, each spring, he cherished their delicate burst of glory.

TURBULENT
TENANTS

S eated in a corner of the local pub, glass of wine perched precariously off-centre on a beer-stained mat, Alice prised her laptop from the rucksack and clicked on WhatsApp to initiate a group call, in the hope that her friends were online. They were.

"Slow down," said Amy, as Alice related her story in as calm a voice as she could muster, which, in all frankness, bordered on hysteria.

"What? Are you serious?" came the stunned response.

"You're insane," was Jack's unflinching contribution. "Ridiculous. Spirits don't exist, except thankfully in bottles."

"Look, I swear, honestly, it's true. The house is haunted. Why would I make it up? Why would I?"

"Well, what does this ghost of yours look like?"

"That's just it. It's kind of invisible. It *does* things."

"Kind of invisible? Does things? What do you mean? Can you be a little more specific?"

"OK. It's… um… thick, cold air, like an almost transparent shadow – hard to explain – and it hurls things round the room, switches lights on and off, fires too – stuff like that."

"Like a poltergeist – *cool!*" exclaimed Amy.

"Not when you're living with one!"

Jack laughed. "Sounds like your imagination's running wild. Do you see it after a night in the pub perhaps?"

"No! And it's *not* my imagination. *No way*. I'm telling you, it exists, and it's pretty intimidating! I might have to look for other accommodation if this continues, but it's so hard to find anywhere this far into term."

"Yes, well-nigh impossible!" rejoined Amy. "Maybe brave it a bit longer then. You've only been there a few days. Things will settle down; there has to be a logical explanation for all of this. I do miss you, but you were so pleased to have discovered such a quaint place. Seems a shame not to give it a chance."

" I suppose you're right," said Alice, not in the least convinced, because her friends, in their cosy little rooms, had no idea, they really didn't.

Halfway through her final year, Alice had decided to move off campus to avoid distractions, such as evenings spent in the student bar and parties, both of which she found hard to resist. So, on discovering an apartment in a house near town, she was over the moon.

The landlady, who resided in a bungalow next door, seemed very keen she take the accommodation.

"It's near the centre and on a bus route to the university," she advertised.

"Yes, that's convenient, and it's got so much character; I can't believe my luck. What a lovely old building. You must have had lots of interest."

The landlady hesitated before replying. "Some."

"How old is it?"

"It was built in the seventeen hundreds."

"Wow! Must be steeped in history. So great! When can I move in?"

"Today if you like," came the brief reply.

"Perfect! Thanks."

The rooms, she noticed, had a rather musty smell to them and they seemed awfully cold, but Alice didn't mind. There was an electric heater in each, which should help cut through the chill. She supposed it was so cold because of the high ceilings – this tended to be the case in big, old properties; she recalled visiting some stately homes, and they were freezing!

The bedroom housed a large bed which dipped in the centre, but that was fine, she would sleep in the middle; and a tall, oak headboard with carved saint-like figurines completed the retro mood.

On a chair nearby lay a folded velvet eiderdown which she hoped would keep her warm at night-time, though its dark maroon colour, she had to admit, was not to her taste. But this was a minor issue; two emerald-green cushions, which she'd recently purchased in a car boot sale, would, no doubt, brighten up the space.

Along a narrow, stone-tiled corridor resided the lounge, the only furniture here (aside from a tired walnut cabinet) being a pair of antique upholstered armchairs, which overshadowed a low, rectangular side table securely sandwiched between them. And resting close by was an old oak desk accompanied by a wooden chair, where she could picture herself settling down to much-needed study.

Then next to this, with its loud, patterned wall tiles and red cupboards glaringly out of sync, a tiny seventies-style kitchen provided a stark contrast to the rest of the decor; yet, despite its exiguous dimensions, it should serve her needs adequately given she wasn't much of a cook and would, no doubt, be ordering takeaway most of the time.

And finally, tucked away at the far end of the building hid a compact bathroom with cast iron bath (its enamel coating chipped from decades of use) and tarnished brass taps. But Alice did not mind these imperfections one bit. This was her new beginning. All was good with the world!

"I've taken it, Amy!" she said. "I'm moving in today. Oh, I nearly forgot – here, have my mobile; I don't want any distractions – none whatsoever! Look after it for me, and if anything important happens, email; I'm taking my laptop, predominantly for research. Oh, and the old record player my dad gave me, and that's it."

"Understood. But no phone! Jesus, Alice, you're crazy!"

"No, not crazy – liberated," replied Alice happily.

"A veritable Luddite – except for the laptop!" grinned Amy. "OK, look, if you're sure that's what you want, go for it. You *will* visit us on campus, though, won't you – maybe next week, just to say hi? You know the old adage: 'All work and no play....'"

She smiled. "Sure, I'll find time, I promise. And if I don't come in person, I'll WhatsApp you. I think I can allow myself just *one* call a week."

And two trips on the bus saw all her worldly

possessions waiting inside the front porch for their apt distribution.

Later that afternoon, having discovered the local launderette, Alice gladly fed her dirty washing into the open jaws of a heavy-duty machine, swiftly transforming its rotating window into a bubbling kaleidoscope of colour.

The presence of her clothes in the laundry bag for the best part of a month, along with a damp, dark-pink towel, had generated a fetid odour rather like a decaying rat; so this unpleasant task finally complete had rendered her nothing short of elated as she happily strolled back to her new abode, a fresh wardrobe of pink-tinged, sweet-smelling garments reflecting her current mood.

On approaching the house, however, something extremely untoward caught her eye, causing her to blink before stopping dead in her tracks. From every single window glared blinding, bright lights like beacons!

"W... what!" she voiced out loud. She was positive she had switched everything off. There must be a good reason for this though, and she refused to allow herself to overthink. It was probably an electrical fault. Yet, on entering the house, she was met too by a red-hot glow issuing from all the fires, which, incredibly, generated no heat whatsoever, as the rooms were cold as ice, and the lights, she noted nervously, were far, far more brilliant than before.

"What in the world!" she exclaimed. "This makes no sense – no sense at all."

But, when Alice knocked on the landlady's door,

the woman did not seem in the least concerned. "Oh, it's happened before – just an electrical fault, due to outdated wiring. Nothing to worry about. I'll contact the electrician."

Her composed response temporarily calmed the girl.

"OK, that's fine. I just wanted to check. Thanks. Sorry for bothering you." And she left, feeling rather foolish.

"There's nothing wrong with the electrics, not that I can see," concluded the electrician the next day. "Might need rewiring at some point but all's fine for now. I've checked the circuits."

"The bar fires don't seem to heat the rooms very effectively," she commented.

"Well, it's to be expected in a large house, dear. Old heating systems are not always as efficient as newer ones. I've got to admit, I didn't know *these* were still in existence." And this said, he left.

Following a meal of sausage, chips and ketchup, closely resembling roadkill, Alice forced herself to study. There was much left to do, and after the recent upheaval, it was time to knuckle down.

Two hours of flicking through sheet upon sheet of handwritten notes – correcting, adding extra points, rereading – had paid off as her finished essay, the first of three, was thankfully now ready to type. And satisfied, she slumped down onto the ancient armchair.

Why she found herself suddenly staring at the wall, she had no idea. But after a while she became aware of a strange, muted shape lurking above the patches of damp which rose with a vengeance from the skirting board – an ominous, almost unseen, force which appeared to be watching her. And she shivered.

"No, it's not real; it's nothing," she chided herself. "Just a shadow."

And, taking a deep breath, she ventured into the kitchen and poured a glass of water. What she witnessed on her return, however, caused her to let out a startled shriek and instantly drop her glass, which plummeted to the hard floor, shattering, like a grenade, into a thousand pieces. Page upon page of notes lay scattered like confetti across the entire room, newly merged with a maelstrom of translucent shards. A terrible shudder coursed through her body, and she stood frozen to the spot.

"My God," she heard herself whisper. "Oh, my God."

Instinctively returning her gaze to the wall, she glimpsed a semi-transparent cloud – a foreboding presence, barely visible, yet somehow solid.

Goosebumps relentlessly invaded her skin like an army of phantom ants and, trembling violently, she grabbed her rucksack and flew to the front entrance, where she frantically twisted the handle of the heavy oak door, before propelling herself onto the garden path. Then tearing round to the landlady's bungalow, she rapped wildly on the door.

"What on earth is the matter?" answered the slightly irritated woman. "I was having my supper."

"There's something in the room… causing havoc. Please help! I don't know what to do," cried Alice breathlessly.

"Well, you need to calm down first. You'd better come in and tell me all about it."

After a frenzied rendition of events had been provided, Alice eagerly awaited advice, clarification, reassurance.

"Look, dear, there's something I should have mentioned."

"What?" came the shaky response.

"It's about the house… there's um… a draft, which surfaces at times, from under the floorboards and doors."

"What do you mean, a draft?"

"Oh, um, it's nothing really – the house is very old and doesn't have the insulation of a modern building."

"So, you're saying the papers were blown over in a draft?"

"Exactly," she concluded. "Nothing at all to worry about."

"The house *is* extremely chilly."

"Yes, and I do apologise for that. If you need an extra blanket, there are some in the wardrobe."

"OK, thanks," responded Alice. "But what about the shadowy form?" she continued.

"Lights on high ceilings often throw shadows, dear, which, with a little imagination, may well seem like something else." And her steely slate-grey eyes fixed steadily on the girl.

"Yes, I guess you're right. Thanks," came the disconcerted reply. Alice remained sceptical as she nervously took her leave, deciding to pop into the local pub for a much-needed drink, and online chat with friends, before bracing herself to return.

The front door had been left wide open (after her fraught exit earlier on) and, taking a deep breath in the hope of achieving composure, she stepped bravely in, closing it behind her. Once in the lounge, she gathered all her notes, strewn like chaff over the hard wooden floor, and arranged them neatly on the table, before placing her laptop, posing as an overgrown paperweight, firmly on top. All fragments of glass were swept up and fed to a largely neglected leather bin, which peeked out guardedly from under the desk, like a wary cat.

Yet, on taking one last look round, she noticed, what she believed to be, a forgotten piece of paper, jutting out slightly from under the cabinet. But as she tentatively attempted to free it from its dusty confines, it refused to move, and a firm tug became necessary for its release. What she now held in her hand, however, was not paper, rather a damp, dusty picture on stretched parchment, of what appeared to be Romans: four faded figurines in flowing, cream-coloured robes. And, without warning, a house spider scurried across the age-stained canvas, causing her to scream inadvertently, thus punctuating the silence. Not choosing to investigate any further, she hastily returned this antiquated object to its former abode.

After a few more glasses of wine were consumed in a vain attempt to calm her nerves, she made straight for the bedroom, feeling sure there had been saint-like figurines on the headboard when she had last looked and, forgetting to take an extra blanket, slipped silently into bed, pulling the eiderdown securely over her head.

A few hours later, it was not the church bells which woke her as they tolled their hourly reminder but instead, loud, classical music resonating discordantly from her record player, which, it should be mentioned, had not as yet been plugged in; and to consider a further noteworthy matter, nor did she have in her possession any classical music! And her fiercely thumping heart became just one more instrument in this macabre rendition, where the grinding strike of the organ threateningly thrashed its way through the startled speakers to torment her.

But alas, this chilling concerto was not all poor Alice was to suffer that night. Within minutes, a decaying, filmy mass floated down onto the bed by her side, causing her eyes to shoot open in sheer terror, coupled with acute revulsion. And pressing its icy form against her quaking body with an invisible might, this grey, fuliginous fog was so close as to smother her in its dense, murky odour, leaving her paralysed – dumbstruck, its deathly soundless mist choking, suffocating, until she knew no more.

When morning came, and mercifully it did, Alice awoke recalling the events of the previous night with appalling clarity. And, after packing her bags with a mechanical urgency, she crept numbly into the lounge to gather up what she could of her remaining belongings, only to behold a profusion of tightly scrunched-up notes littering the floor, like discarded ping-pong balls; and the robed Romans, semi-transparent, hovered in mid-air like bubbles, their blank canvas home lying on the floor, awaiting their return.

Seconds later, releasing the heavy bags from her vice-like grip, she found herself knocking frantically on the landlady's door. Her thunderous pummelling, however, was met by silence. In vain, Alice continued to strike the door, but to no avail. Then, hearing a neighbour opening her window, she turned and hastened towards her.

"What are you doing here?" called out the woman.

"I need to speak to the landlady to tell her I'm leaving – right now!"

"She's not in. I saw her going to the shops. No doubt she'll be back soon. I don't like her. Come inside; your face is as white as a sheet."

Alice obeyed, allowing herself to be led into the dusty, disorganised room. And, temporarily forgetting her recent trauma, she said: "Oh, how wonderfully warm it is in here." Yet she still shivered uncontrollably.

"You're in shock; I can see that." And the woman, shifting in her chair, listened while the poor girl blurted out her chilling narrative.

"This doesn't distress me as much as you might think; I'm used to shock. Let me tell you about the old tales passed down over generations. They suggest that the house was constructed on an ancient burial ground, thus disturbing, and angering, the long dead."

Alice listened intently.

"My friend Elsie," she continued, "I liked Elsie… moved into her bungalow about thirty years since and, on numerous occasions, could discern loud, plaintive moaning emerging from that woefully unholy house – always at night-time – and she witnessed dazzling lights, too, like you spoke of, flashing from every window.

Naturally, these eerie episodes upset her, but like she said: 'That's why I got the place so cheap – beggars can't be choosers, Mabel,' – that's my name, Mabel. What's yours?"

"Alice," replied the girl in a whisper.

"So, like I said, the hauntings were no secret; back then, everyone knew about them, and everyone who has lived in that godforsaken place has been traumatised – or worse. In the early seventies, I recall, it was occupied by an old man, a recluse and poet, who wrote about strange presences, hideous apparitions; and one evening, Elsie found him, pale and shivering on the steps; and in hushed tones, he revealed that his poems had been ripped to shreds, thus destroying the ghastly truth. She told me he'd mumbled, in a barely audible voice, that it was all too late, before retreating into the house. Sadly, later that week, he slit both his wrists."

"How dreadful!" replied Alice, shuddering.

"Yes. And, one day, the council decided to plant some trees on the land behind the house, little knowing—"

"What? Little knowing, what?" she asked anxiously.

"Little knowing that the patch of land was a part of the burial ground. And they discovered human remains – skulls and bones; sherds of pottery and precious stones were dug up too. Detectives came to investigate, and the area was cordoned off. Anyway, to cut a long story short, the findings were analysed by experts and the evidence revealed that they dated back to as long ago as Roman times."

Alice trembled as she recalled the picture. "So, what became of Elsie?" she hurriedly continued. "I spoke to a woman, who appeared to be the landlady, when I first arrived and just the other day too."

There was a long pause, before Mabel spoke.

"Elsie, bless her heart… well, the hauntings, and the poet's suicide, started to affect her sanity; she used to wander around in the middle of the night, scared out of her wits – lost her marbles in the end. She died a few months ago when her sister moved in. I don't like her sister. I don't like her."

"So, her sister is the landlady now?" Alice could not help wondering what the sister had done to deserve Mabel's wrath.

"Yes, her twin sister, Ellen, not a nice person, and she's no business renting that dreadful place." And Mabel's face became pale, her expression stony. "No business whatsoever, putting poor people, like you, in danger; someone needs to sort her out, it's a disgrace."

"Well, thanks for telling me all this," replied Alice, choosing to ignore Mabel's last remark. "It makes more sense now, if that's the right word, and it's nice to know I'm not crazy after all."

"Course not. Anyhow, she's back now. I see her from the window."

"OK, I'd best be off. It was nice meeting you." And she strode purposefully in the direction of the bungalow.

"Can I help you?" questioned the landlady, noting the girl's indignation.

"Yes. I'm leaving," came the angry response. "You should have told me the truth about this place! Not made me feel I was being hysterical."

"Would you have rented, if I had?"

"Of course not!"

"Exactly! I do need to make a living, you know," she replied bluntly.

"Yes, at other people's psychological expense." And Alice, still in shock, picked up her luggage and left for the bus.

On arrival at the university, she immediately rushed to Amy's room, throwing herself into her friend's warm arms.

"Oh my God, Alice, you're shaking furiously! And you're deathly pale... and so very, very cold... like ice. Whatever happened to you? Are you OK?"

Over the ensuing weeks, Amy's concern for her friend, who was still acutely affected by her recent trauma, had escalated. Often, on observing Alice, whose complexion since her fraught return had grown waxy and pallid, she noticed that the girl appeared lost... alone... and had taken to gazing vacantly out of the window, far across the fields, towards the town, as if in a trance... as if an invisible force were beckoning her.

"I'm worried about you, Alice," she said, eventually. "You don't seem your old self. You have to report that awful woman. The local authorities need to be alerted. *And...* you should definitely take a break."

"Yes, believe me, I know. My counsellor advised the very same," sighed the girl. "I'll go at the weekend. I promise. I'll catch a train and escape to the coast."

"Yes, and oust those dreadful demons once and for all!" asserted Amy.

"Here's hoping," replied Alice quietly. And a faint, yet steady smile stole over her pale lips.

The next day, insisting on anonymity, Alice had agreed, albeit hesitantly, to send a letter regarding the entire story of the haunted house, disclosing, in detail, an account of the neighbour's disturbing tales; so that, in future, the landlady would be legally obliged to inform prospective tenants that the premises were haunted and potentially dangerous. And, once complete, she signed it simply – A.

Following a thorough investigation by local officials, however, including the press and an interested police inspector, the report finally came back denoting the nearby bungalow had been boarded up in 1977, and later demolished, after the brutal murder of its owner, Elsie Ellen, by her neighbour, Mabel. And subsequently, due to a severe psychotic disorder, the latter was given a court verdict of 'diminished responsibility' before being placed in a psychiatric hospital in the countryside, where she later died.

And the big old house, its antiquated rooms coated in cobwebs and thick dust, seemed not to have been lived in since the early seventies, judging by the kitchen decor pertaining to this period. Yet, in stark disparity, two nearly new and extremely bright, emerald-green cushions, dotted with saint-like figurines, their corners gnawed by hungry rats, were discovered strewn over the bedroom floor, their spilled stuffing faintly fashioned in the shape of a letter 'A'. While nearby, a frail, forsaken record player, encrusted in age-old grime, leaned, sad and mute, against the damp wall. The lounge, ice-cold like the other rooms, was peppered with myriad shards of broken glass, and under the cabinet, on ancient parchment, a painting of four Romans was unearthed, in the corner of which, scrawled in blood, was a verse from a poem, dated, strangely, many centuries later in 1972, which read:

'Seize your wings,
Make haste, be gone!
Too late for me,
My wings are stone.
A darkness
Has engulfed me,
I scream alone...!'

A DAY ON THE ISLAND

"Don't you dare mount that dear little donkey with your heavy rucksack!" warned Vita, tenderly stroking the animal's soft head. "Poor thing looks exhausted."

"*Seriously*! *I'm* exhausted! I can't trudge up all these millions of steps in such blistering heat."

"The donkey has to!"

"Yes, I know – poor donkey, but not poor Pavlos, I notice! OK, but you can buy me a drink at the top; that's if I ever reach the top!"

"You're such a drama queen, but fine, I'll buy you a drink and treat you to lunch."

"Thank you. I suddenly sense a spurt of energy flooding through me. I just might make it."

Such idyllic islands must surely have been blessed by the hand of God. She was in heaven, and the liquid door to the deep underwater paradise, its vibrant, verdant-blue reflection reaching out to the warm, golden shore, was a testimony to this. To live here forever would be bliss. Yes. A small, whitewashed house, with bougainvillea hugging the walls; not forgetting a resident cat, naturally! Learn Greek, of course. Brightly coloured terracotta pots, with orange-red geraniums sprouting energetically from the fertile soil… perfection epitomised!

"Hey, Vita, come on, stop daydreaming. We've got another thousand steps yet before we can relax! Oh, and look, that man who is now riding comfortably up the hill on the very same donkey is about twice the size of me!"

"That's awful, there should be a weight limit! But at least *we* didn't add to the poor animal's hardship; it's the principal at the end of the day."

"Yes, and it'll be the end of the day by the time we climb up all these steps! *And… just saying…* but that donkey would have been considerably less distressed had skinny little me ridden it in the first place."

Half an hour of intense heat later, the two breathless friends appeared at the top of the hill, marvelling at the magnificent vista below. A far cry from home with its traffic, city air and 'let's-make-the-most-of-it' weather!

Minute boats, their sails like happy lungs gratefully inhaling the deliciously salt-fresh air, and white ferries like floating seagulls, all gently bobbed up and down in this vast aquatic garden which was their home.

"Thanks for inviting me, Pav. I'm so glad we came," she said simply.

"Me too," he smiled. "Come on, let's eat."

At the nearest local restaurant, a delicious lunch of tzatziki and octopus salad, accompanied by a huge glass of iced water, was readily consumed by the excited, albeit dehydrated, pair as they slumped gratefully on painted cerulean chairs, by a round wooden table, and basked in the Mediterranean sun.

"What did he say?" she asked, hearing Pavlos speaking in Greek.

"Oh, the waiter mentioned if we're looking for accommodation, he has a room in a nearby village," he explained. "It's his lunch break now, so he can take us, if we're interested."

"Sounds great. It means we don't have to waste this beautiful afternoon searching for somewhere to stay. We can head for the beach instead."

"I'll tell him we'll take it then."

"Yeah, why not."

Struggling to keep up with their strapping guide, they climbed ever further up the hill until the village gradually came into view, and the striking cluster of bright-white buildings dazzled them in the glorious sunlight.

"How beautiful!" she gasped, and the man smiled proudly.

"He says he's lived here all his life," translated Pavlos.

"What a wonderful place to grow up in," she sighed.

"Yes. Oh, and he needs to have our passports."

"What for?"

"For security – to ensure the place doesn't get damaged, that kind of stuff. It's how things are done here."

"I guess that's fine then," replied Vita, pulling the document from her rucksack. "Good job you speak Greek; we wouldn't have got this otherwise."

"Glad to be of service," he grinned, clutching a giant key dangling heavily, like a sluggish sloth, from a string of worry beads.

Seconds later, though, after a brief nod, their guide promptly disappeared down the hill.

"Where's he gone?" asked the girl, somewhat bewildered.

"He had to get back for his next shift. So from here we simply follow his directions."

"Great! He took our passports and now he's abandoned us."

"Oh, you of little faith. It's all good; he assured me the house is near and easy to find; it has a bright-blue hibiscus by the wall and a Greek flag on the gate."

Several thin, dusty tracks and sandy oleander-dotted lanes later, the over-heated pair, powdery sand smudging their flip-flops and beads of sweat sprouting from their foreheads, had still not arrived. A mangy cat, with knotted fur and crusted sleep in its eyes, drew lazily near, meowing lethargically before swishing its matted tail against their damp legs; but albeit grubby and flea-bitten, Vita noted, it was certainly not emaciated, due, no doubt, to honed hunting skills and the kindness of humans.

"Finally!" came Pavlos' sudden and elated cry, inducing the now-nervous animal to dive headfirst into a nearby bush. "There's the shrub, awash with blue… and the flag on the gate!" he declared. "Yes, this is definitely it!" And Vita perched gratefully on the whitewashed wall.

"How picturesque!" she exclaimed, gazing out to sea. "The view from up here is priceless. Quite hard to find though… all the houses look the same."

"Yeah true," he agreed, unlocking the ancient, blue door with, indubitably, the bulkiest key he had ever encountered.

The room was extremely basic, with threadbare towels and rusty taps, and there was just one very small window and a picture of Jesus high on a stone wall. And, hiding behind the door, jutting out from another wall, lay two narrow, solid structures, also of stone, with thin mattresses and flat pillows flung loosely on top. But, while this awfully stark setting rendered her a touch uneasy, she was sure it would suffice for one night; and Pavlos seemed happy enough. So, throwing down their bags and selecting towels, swimsuits and sun cream, they left.

The afternoon was spent at an idyllic beach, which was virtually empty, and the overheated friends gladly stripped off and jumped into the refreshing, fish-laden sea.

"They're nipping my ankle," she giggled.

"The fish like you – *or* the nip is a mere taste before they sink their razor-sharp fangs into your succulent, flavoursome flesh."

"Very funny! Well, I'm going with the former. And I like them too."

"It's great here, isn't it," he sighed happily.

"Yes, heavenly."

And, gently bowing their heads, they peered through the watery window of this hidden world, with its minute sea creatures tucked up cosily in tiny rock pools, shrouded by ribbons of olive-green seaweed, and gazed at miniature silver fish flashing, like fleeting moments, over the shimmering bed of white pebbles, in the shady sanctuary of their private palace.

The next three blissful hours of pure tranquillity found the couple lying stretched out on the warm rocks like basking otters, fast asleep; this explained why the sudden frenzied shouting, which cut like a knife through their repose, took them both by complete surprise. And jolting bolt upright, Vita glimpsed a stern old woman storming purposefully towards her with, she noted, extremely sturdy legs for someone who must, without a doubt, have been in their eighties, at the very least. Not yet understanding, the girl offered a shy smile, but, in a flash, the irate lady lunged forward, waving her hands in the air, like frantic wings, over Vita's breasts, crying: "*Ochi, ochi!*"[3]

"Get away from me!" came the instinctive, if somewhat fearful, reply, before Pavlos provided much-needed enlightenment.

"Better put your top on, quick," he urged. "You're upsetting the locals. This isn't a tourist beach, and your nakedness is considered offensive."

"Oh, God. Sorry." And now comprehending fully, her face became as red as a tomato, and she hurriedly dressed.

"*Sygnomi,*"[4] apologised Pavlos, and the woman, slightly calmer now, marched away, the rim of her sun hat flapping in synchrony with her shaking head.

"I didn't realise."

"Don't worry, it's fine. Quite funny actually. Your face was a picture when she tried to grab your breasts," he laughed.

---

3   ochi (oxi) – no.
4   sygnomi – sorry.

And after a hasty departure, they managed, not without difficulty, to negotiate the maze of tapering lanes back to their room, before washing under a precariously positioned trickling tap, which failed feebly to impersonate a showerhead.

Setting out a while later, clad in light evening attire, the pair made for the town, in eager anticipation of discovering the island's nightlife. And they were far from disappointed. The surprisingly vibrant atmosphere, given the compact square, delighted our two tourists, who purchased an extremely well-endowed figurine of the god, Priapus, and a turquoise-stone ring, before savouring fresh sea bass accompanied by locally produced wine in a cosy seafront restaurant.

And a few hours in, they found themselves watching the sun set from the rooftop terrace of a brightly lit bar, where they danced to Greek music spilling from big, black speakers adorned with fairy lights and sipped pink cocktails, Greek style, hence hugely generous measures.

In time, as was foreseeable, the sparkling lights became somewhat hazy and blurry and the world a little swirly, like a spinning top.

"I think I've had enough," confessed Vita.

"Me too," agreed Pavlos, adding, "but maybe just *one* more before we head home?"

"Yes, why not indeed! I do love you, you know."

"You too, almost as much as that beautiful waiter over there," he joked.

"Ooo, handsome." And the girl reached unsteadily

for her drink. "I actually feel I could fly right now," she giggled.

"Well, please don't, because you really can't."

"OK, never mind – this pink and blue drink tastes divine. Is the parasol edible, do you think?"

"God, Vita, how much have you had?" But, after a brief pause, he laughed out loud. "The same as me, I guess! I shouldn't have suggested that last one. Come on, time to go."

Stars dotted the inky surface of the night sky as the friends meandered along the spindly, ill-lit tracks, leaning one on the other for much-needed support. Locating the village appeared easy. However, tracing their accommodation was another matter entirely.

"None of the houses are lit up. It's so very dark," whispered Pavlos, nervously running his fingers through his dark, curly hair. "I have no idea where we are."

Vita shivered. "Feels like a ghost town – so silent."

"Yes, and our room could be anywhere; it'd be like searching for a needle in a haystack; I wouldn't know where to start."

"Well let's sit right here and think about it," she suggested, helpfully flopping down on the grass.

Yet even when presented with such an appealing proposal, Pavlos remained adamant they seek out their elusive shelter, and within seconds they were staggering along a labyrinth of sandy lanes to recommence their search.

But, sadly to no avail. The village, a dusk-kissed mountain, was bespeckled with barely visible blue doors and shutters etched into its shadowy surface.

Clearly, they had set themselves an insurmountable task.

Nevertheless, after what seemed an eternity, Vita cried out, "Wait! That's it. I remember the cross above the door – it looks like a chapel! Oh God, I didn't realise before, but it *is* a chapel! We can't sleep *here*."

"Why on earth not! We've as good as paid for it."

And, so saying, Pavlos unlocked the door and fumbled around for a light switch, eventually discovering a length of cord, which he deduced, in the absence of anything else, must be it. When he tugged, however, nothing happened, not even a reassuring click could be heard.

"Stupid thing won't work!" he groaned. "We'll have to sleep in the dark."

"No, I don't like this one bit!" she exclaimed. "It's eerie with these tomb-like beds. I bet they even are tombs. And it's pitch-black too! I don't want to stay here. We can't spend the night in a church! Let's grab our stuff and sleep under the stars."

And without requiring any further persuasion, he concurred. Clothes were blindly fished for, thrown into bags and the door slammed swiftly behind them. The steep lanes proved strenuous to navigate, but after a while, catching her breath, Vita spoke.

"I swear we've been here before. We've come full circle. I remember this field on the side of the hill."

"You're right. D'you know what, let's settle here on the grass verge."

"We could have done this an hour ago!" And grumbling, yet at the same time relieved, she plonked herself down a second time.

The night air was noticeably cooler. And a thick cover of darkness masked their surroundings, but despite the cold, and due to drink and weariness, sleep came effortlessly.

It was not until early morning that Vita was awoken by a loud din – a mixture of distressed duck and angry wolf – and unable to suitably identify the sound, she panicked, shaking her companion mercilessly.

"There's a wild beast out there! Could be a… oh I don't know, a werewolf or something! Get up quickly! Pav, get up!"

"W… what? Werewolf? Joking, right! Your imagination surpasses you. Look, it's probably a cow or goat; go back to sleep."

As the commotion had now subsided, she took his advice. Not long afterwards, however, she was roused again, by a warm, wettish, almost slimy, sensation, like a slug trail on her neck. Cautiously opening her eyes, she witnessed a donkey nuzzling her affectionately and, on still closer scrutiny, came the realisation that this was the very same donkey from the day before. It had reached as far as the rope which tethered it would allow in order to kiss her.

"You little darling. What are the odds we'd meet again?" she said sotto voce. "Was it you making all that racket earlier?"

The sun gradually rose, framing the animal's head in an orange-red light, and this beautiful portrait, with a halo-like glow, seemed almost sacred – an epiphany – and she felt humbled.

Tracking down their landlord later that morning proved far less trouble; he was happily installed in his local café engaged in animated dialogue, a Metaxa and Greek coffee perched on the miniature blue table in front of him.

"Let's appeal to his better nature," suggested Vita. "He might give us discount, 'cause, to be honest, he did pull a fast one, didn't he?"

But, after listening with a marked lack of interest to their complaints, the man stressed that this was really not his problem. And a rather lively discussion ensued.

"He says if we want our passports, we must pay in full," grumbled Pavlos frustratedly. "No payment, no passports!"

"OK, that's pretty conclusive, I guess. Never mind, at least we tried. You might want to work on your bargaining skills for next time, though. Come on, let's go. Oh, and I must buy some carrots."

"Carrots? Could have done with those last night," he laughed. "Might not have got lost."

"Listen, I need your help. It could benefit the donkeys, who knows? Let me explain." And her plan was duly revealed.

At the top of the steep steps to the ferry boat, she stopped the gruff, old man in charge of the animals, notifying him, via Pavlos' translation, of the holy vision she had witnessed on the previous night, followed by an extra rendition of her own making.

"I have no idea how religious you are, but I'm informing you that this donkey," and she indicated, "is blessed. Last night I had a vision: I saw a halo appear over his head, and I heard a celestial voice descend from the heavens ordering that he be revered: 'Hallowed be my animals,' it said. And a name was spoken: 'Stavros.'"

"That's my name," said the man quietly.

"Oh – is it? Heavens above, it must be a sign! Anyway, I'll never forget such a wondrous moment – formidable, one which will bide with me forever – so I considered it my moral duty to impart this divine message, to ensure all the island's donkeys are well nurtured and at no point subjected to excessive load-bearing. I've brought refreshments for them." And so saying, she placed some bottled water on the white-stone steps, before handing him the carrots. And embracing the little donkey affectionately, she smiled at the bemused handler, who remained silent, if a tad uneasy, bag of carrots dangling loosely by his side.

"Well, I tried my best," she said as they walked away. "Who knows, it might have made a difference?"

"Or he might have deemed you certifiable!"

"Well, he didn't laugh me off the island – that's got to count for something. He might believe in stuff like that; a lot of people do – I do, in a way. Oh, and thanks for translating so effectively."

"My pleasure. Your story was very convincing. How did you know his name?"

"I heard someone call it out when we first arrived."

"Clever!"

"We had fun here, didn't we."

"Yes, we certainly did. So, where next?" he smiled, as they descended the many steps (on foot, naturally) to the waiting boat.

THE QUEUE

Lilly, just turned eighteen, and lumbered with small child screaming blue murder, was third in line. A couple of months ago, she had unwittingly rung a loan company, oblivious of their notoriously seedy reputation, and the five hundred pounds she had initially borrowed, thus enabling her to meet rental requirements, had fast become more due to excessive amounts of interest which were being demanded on a weekly basis. Certainly, she should have known better, but desperation had been at the helm of this foolhardy and misguided action.

Unsuccessfully struggling to swim above water, she had sunk into a deep depression, coupled with anxiety, which was currently exacerbated by the incessant hollering of her two-year-old, who refused point-blank to trade better behaviour for sweets and a toy car.

Shuffling from side to side, her longing for a cigarette mounting, Lilly impatiently adjusted her pale-blue disposable mask and sighed. She had observed that people seemed to be ignoring the sign advocating mask wearing, so, without much procrastinating, opted to remove her own.

Only yesterday, she'd had her third Covid-19

vaccination, and the groggy after-effects were hitting hard. Desperate not to cough, because people looked at you funnily these days, she swallowed and held her breath, until she felt near to passing out.

Shut up, child, for pity's sake, shut up! she longed to say.

Everyone was eyeing her, disapprovingly shaking their heads at a mother who allowed all this terrible din, and she wished to tear down these twitching curtains of rebuke and punch a few noses, figuratively speaking; however, clutching on to a modicum of composure, she desisted.

"Shh, quieten down, Charlie. We'll be home soon," she said instead.

Home. That was a laugh. The aforementioned loan sharks had invited themselves in the other day while she was at the supermarket, oblivious of their intent; they'd taken her TV and microwave and trashed the house, which now looked as if a hurricane had struck. She, and her toddler, were alone. No dad – he disappeared with the money she kept in a turquoise vase on the top shelf. She had no idea he had any knowledge of her secreted cash. No idea at all. But it turns out he did. A gold bracelet, gifted by her mother before she left for a holiday in Australia, had also gone AWOL.

And, as the wait persisted, the girl, unable to contain herself for another second, eventually exploded like a shaken soda can: "For God's sake, can't you get someone else on the desk; I've been waiting for ages! It's not good enough. I can't stand here all day! I have things to do."

"Sorry, madam, everyone's busy," replied the clerk,

her slight traces of irritability efficiently obscured by a lethargically limp apology.

"*I'm* busy, as well, you know!" shouted Lilly, her irrevocable frustration growing by the second. "*Everyone's busy!*" And, so saying, she flicked her hair back abruptly and burst into tears.

Daniel, next in line, wanted to put his arm around her, to comfort her, but she was a stranger and he deemed it inappropriate, so, as an ineptly chosen alternative, he smiled helplessly.

"What are you staring at?" she cried out. "Think this is funny, do you! *You* try taking care of a two-year-old, twenty-four seven! Bloody men!"

"Oh, no… I was just… smiling, nothing more," he muttered, taken aback.

"Well, get lost will you! Creep."

All his previous thoughts had now been well and truly crushed by this rebuff. He had been relaxing on the river, rowing his boat, skimming past the tall, wispy reeds, listening to the calm ripples of the water awash with lily pads and ducks, absorbed in birdsong. How he loved this virtual place; no one in sight, a luxurious tranquillity. But not anymore. His peace had suddenly been shattered; his boat hopelessly entangled in the reeds. Mortified that she had misunderstood his innocent concern, deeming him nothing short of some sort of reprobate, he hung his head.

A good half hour later, the girl remained number three in the queue. Her nerves were glass fragments, and her desire to smoke – and, ironically, breathe fresh air – pierced her like a pinpoint.

"Are you OK?" enquired Daniel bravely, noting her increasing angst.

"No, I'm not, actually! What's it to you anyway?"

"I just thought," he ventured, "that if you need to go outside for a breather, I could keep an eye on your child."

A brisk pause ensued, where the insult she had prepared slid safely away.

"OK, thanks; I'll only be a minute."

His relief at being elevated from predator to saviour, was marked.

"Great. I'll call you if your turn comes. Take as long as you want."

And she did.

In her absence, Daniel related fascinating adventures of pandas (reminiscent of his trip to Australia), bears (taken from *Winnie the Pooh*) and fairies (Tinkerbell); he formed faces, gestures, antic voices, and the previously screaming child was silent... if a trifle perplexed, wondering who exactly this overzealous, crazy clown was. Yet in the absence of his mother, he decided, on balance, to give his personal storyteller a chance. And only now and then did he turn his head, in hopeful anticipation, towards the door.

Nearly twenty minutes later, Lilly returned and smiled at the pair.

"Thank you so much," she said, apologising for her prior tetchiness.

What a lovely face she had, mused Daniel, such kindness under that mask of irritability, defensiveness and frustration. And he watched her flick back her long hair, gently this time, not angrily as before.

"Have you ever been on a boat?" he asked, attempting further connection.

"Once. One of those peddle boats, it was shaped like a swan. I went with my mum when I was a kid. She bought me an ice cream – Cornish with clotted cream and blackcurrant sauce… delicious!" she said, basking in the memory.

"Sounds wonderful."

And they chatted avidly regarding pleasurable topics – music, favourite foods, films – while discussing too, the not so agreeable, such as loan sharks and debt.

"Anyway, I've decided to pay them off in full; that's why I'm here," she explained. "I'd rather have a hefty overdraft with the bank than ever get mixed up in that shady business again."

"Wise decision. Make sure you have someone with you, though, as backup."

"Yes, my brother will help for sure; he's good like that, and his best friend's a cop, so that could well come in handy."

Confiding in this man, whose face creased slightly with concentration – concern too – was effortless, and his earnest demeanour she found nothing short of charming. No one had listened to her like this, with such empathy, indeed benevolence, in a very long time; to be valued – noticed even – lifted her spirits, and when her turn finally arrived, unsurprisingly, she did not hear the clerk call: "Next, please."

"Excuse me, madam, you're next," repeated the newly agitated woman, in a rather more emphatic tone.

"Oh, OK, coming."

"Do you fancy meeting up some time?" he asked, not wanting her to go.

"Yes," came the reply. "I'll give you my number when I've finished."

"What about a meal out?"

"Are you joking? With a two-year-old?"

"A picnic in the park? Maybe row down the river?" he suggested, hopefully.

"More like it! Yes, that'd be fun."

"Brilliant," he answered, with a semblance of calmness, not wishing to appear too enthusiastic too soon and thus wreck things. But his heart beat fiercely in his chest.

"Could you hurry, madam, there are people still queueing."

Lilly did not answer back this time, although one could have forgiven her for doing so, given the lengthy delay. And as she conversed with the clerk, her voice took on a light, chirpy tone, causing Charlie to look round, and a happy glow, so long denied, lit up her face like magic.

ABOUT THE AUTHOR

Vivien Varga has worked as an English and Drama teacher in Warwickshire and the West Midlands and lived for several years in Bologna. She now spends her time travelling and writing. 'Marika' is her first book, inspired by her mother's stories of her childhood and wartime experiences, 'A perfect Ending and Other Stories', her second.

This book is printed on paper from sustainable sources managed under the Forest Stewardship Council (FSC) scheme.

It has been printed in the UK to reduce transportation miles and their impact upon the environment.

For every new title that Matador publishes, we plant a tree to offset CO_2, partnering with the More Trees scheme.

For more about how Matador offsets its environmental impact, see www.troubador.co.uk/about/